His gaze turned incendiary. "You lost your chance to set the rules of the game when you elected to keep your pregnancy from me, Sofía."

He knew. She swallowed hard and forced herself to stay calm. "I was going to tell you. This week."

"This week?" Nikandros yelled the words, his iron control snapping. "Do you have *any* idea what this means?"

Her insides flip-flopped. "Of course I do. Which is why I haven't said anything yet. Because I knew you would appear just like you have now and start making decisions. And I need to understand how *I* feel about this first. What *I* want to do."

His gaze narrowed on her. "What you want *to do*?"

Heat rushed to her cheeks. "I didn't mean that. Of course I'm having this baby. It's the logistics I'm not sure of."

"*Logistics* we should have discussed days ago."

She stared at Nikandros. Did he think this was any more convenient for her, with her lifestyle? Any less than a disaster for her than it was for him?

Her chin dipped. "We can talk about this over the phone."

He caught her jaw in his fingers, the rage burning in his eyes making her heart pound.

"We aren't talking ab
law says
to the thr
solve *no*

Jennifer Hayward invites you into a world of…

Kingdoms & Crowns

Young royals in reckless pursuit of passion!

When a centuries-old battle between the kingdoms of
Akathinia and Carnelia is reignited the nation's young
royals find themselves on the brink of war. But their
kingdoms aren't the only thing at stake…

Soon these young monarchs are facing an
unexpected royal baby, the appearance of a
lost princess and an alliance with the enemy.

Can love conquer all?

Find out in:

King Nikandros and Sofia Ramirez's story
Carrying the King's Pride
March 2016

Look for:

Princess Alexandra and Aristos Nicolades's story

and

King Kostas and Princess Stella's story

Coming soon from Mills & Boon Modern Romance!

CARRYING THE KING'S PRIDE

BY
JENNIFER HAYWARD

Published in Great Britain 2016
By Mills & Boon, an imprint of HarperCollins*Publishers*
1 London Bridge Street, London, SE1 9GF

© 2016 Jennifer Drogell

ISBN: 978-0-263-91595-2

Our policy is to use papers that are natural, renewable and recyclable products and made from wood grown in sustainable forests. The logging and manufacturing processes conform to the legal environmental regulations of the country of origin.

Printed and bound in Spain
by CPI, Barcelona

Jennifer Hayward has been a fan of romance since filching her sister's novels to escape her teenage angst. Her career in journalism and PR—including years of working alongside powerful, charismatic CEOs and travelling the world—has provided her with perfect fodder for the fast-paced, sexy stories she likes to write—always with a touch of humour. A native of Canada's east coast, Jennifer lives in Toronto with her Viking husband and young Viking-in-training.

Visit the Author Profile page at millsandboon.co.uk for more titles.

For my mother, who is quite simply the best person I know. Your spirit and love of philosophy inspired this book. Your belief in me has always been such a big part of how I get to 'The End'.

And for Stella, for your help and for being one of those people you meet once and know it can't be for the last time.

CHAPTER ONE

Sofía Ramirez put a Manolo Blahnik–clad toe out of the classic yellow Manhattan taxi, her shoe meeting pavement still radiating heat from a sultry, steamy New York summer day.

She followed up the iconic shoe with a slim leg that caused a tuxedo-clad male on the sidewalk to turn and watch, a champagne-colored, beaded cocktail dress that accentuated her voluptuous figure without flaunting it and a Kate Spade clutch a shade deeper than her dress.

Suitably assembled on the sidewalk, she paid the driver, ran a palm over her sleek French twist to make sure it was intact and made her way toward the entrance of the glimmering, stately Metropolitan Museum of Art.

As the co-owner of one of Manhattan's trendiest fashion boutiques, she knew the importance of dressing for the occasion. Overdress in this city and you looked as if you were trying too hard. Underdress and you would be talked about all night by the highbrow crowd.

She thought she'd gotten it just right as she swished through the front doors of the museum, where one of her most important clients was hosting a benefit for the arts. But could any outfit ever really prepare a woman for her other, perhaps more important, task of the evening—

saying thanks, but no thanks, to her relationship with one of Manhattan's most powerful men?

Not just a man. A prince. The sexy, charismatic second in line to the throne of his tiny Mediterranean kingdom, Akathinia, Prince Nikandros Constantinides, in attendance tonight. *The untamable one*, as the women who had dated him were wont to say in quick sound bites to the press, the slight hint of bitterness to their tone the only outward sign they were in any way chastened at being yet another of his castoffs.

For didn't they all know their time with the prince was limited to the length of his attention span? That once his interest wandered, the clock was on?

She had known it. And what had she done? Waited for him to call when he'd come back from Mexico, his much-lauded free trade deal in hand, obsessively checking her phone for a message from him every fifteen minutes only to find nothing until tonight when he'd known they would be at the same party.

Her stomach curled with a fresh burst of nerves as she handed her invitation to the greeters at the door of the Egyptian-themed Temple of Dendur exhibit. Getting herself into a state over a man, even one as gorgeous as Nik, was something she'd sworn she'd never do. Couldn't allow herself to do. So she was going to do what any smart, sensible woman would in her situation.

End it. Cut it off before he broke her heart. Before he made her want things she couldn't have. Things she'd long ago determined weren't attainable for her.

Her attendance verified, she wound her way through the glitzy, bejeweled crowd to look for her hostess, Natalia Graham, a well-respected philanthropist who came from one of Manhattan's historic, moneyed families. Business first, heart-pounding personal matter later.

The Temple of Dendur, a gift to the United States from Egypt in the late 1960s, then bequeathed to the Met, was lit up this evening as the centerpiece of the event. Harkening back to the age of the pharaohs and the gods they worshipped, it was breathtaking.

Several acquaintances stopped her to talk, all of them clients. She spent a few moments with each, summoning the polite small talk she had studiously taught herself over the years, because when you came from the opposite side of town these people did, where this world had once only been a dream in your daily existence, you weren't equipped with those skills.

"Sofia." Natalia found her moments later, drawing her into a warm embrace. "I'm so glad you made it."

"I'm sorry I'm late. It was a crazy day."

"And you probably want off your feet." Natalia drew her toward the bar. "No Katharine tonight?"

She shook her head at the mention of her partner. "Her father is in town."

"And no gorgeous man to escort you?" Natalia gave her a wry look. "I would have thought the men would be lining up to date you. Unless," her friend said slyly, "the rumors of you and the prince are true?"

"I don't have time to date," she said smoothly, sliding onto a bar stool. "You know I'm always working."

"Mmm." Natalia gave her a speculative look. "Martini?"

"Please." A healthy shot of potent alcohol might go a long way toward the liquid courage she needed at the moment.

She and Natalia caught up, working their way around to the joint endeavor they had been planning, a fashion show in support of one of Natalia's charities. They were discussing the details when the philanthropist's gaze sharpened on the crowd behind them.

"Speaking of the prince," she drawled, "he just sat down behind you."

Her pulse picked up, thrumming a steady beat in her throat. A prickly sensation slid up her back. She didn't need to turn around to know Nik had spotted her. She could feel the heat of his gaze, eating her up as it always did.

"Well, I guess that answers my question," Natalia murmured.

Sofía took a sip of her martini. She and Nik had managed to keep their relationship out of the tabloids after they'd met at a hospital fund-raiser, but rumors had been circulating of late. Since their relationship would be dead after tonight, she saw no reason to confirm it to Natalia.

"It's nothing." She shrugged. "You know what he's like."

Natalia lifted a brow. "If that's his *it's nothing* look, I'd like to see the *something* one."

She dug her teeth into her lip. Unable to resist, she swiveled on the stool, directing her gaze toward the group of men populating the lounge area behind them. It didn't take her long to locate Nik. Tall, dark and swarthy-skinned in a nod to his Mediterranean heritage, he looked…breathtaking.

The jacket of his silver-gray suit lay discarded on the back of his seat as per the jackets of the other men at the table, his white shirt open at the throat, his every physical cue as he lounged, long legs spread out in front of him, that of supreme confidence.

Her stomach twisted, her agitation intensifying. He looked like sex poured into an exquisitely made suit. Lethally powerful. *Dangerous.*

She lifted her gaze to his light, magnetic one that contrasted so vividly with his olive skin. Blue, an icy blue, it was focused on her in a not-so-discreet perusal, full of a sensual promise that took her breath away.

A wave of heat consumed her. He was just that *virile*.

Turning around, she reached for her glass and took a long sip with a hand that trembled ever so slightly. *Remember how discarded, how vulnerable you felt waiting for him to call this week.* That had to be her armor tonight.

You are going to do this, Sofía. You are not going to back out again. Muster your willpower.

"Bar bill says she will."

"You're on."

Nik pulled his attention away from Sofía and frowned at his two closest friends. "What's the wager for?"

"You." Harry, his best friend since college, flicked him an amused smile. "I bet the bar bill the eye candy over there breaks your self-imposed slump. Jake says she doesn't."

Nik could have told him she already had. That he and Sofía had been seeing each other for a couple of months. But he liked things the way they were. Private. *Uncomplicated.* Sizzling hot.

He took a sip of his whiskey, savoring the smoky flavor of the spirit before pointing his glass at Harry. "I've spent the past six months negotiating a free trade deal. A *landmark* free trade deal, I might add. It's not a slump. It's a lack of bandwidth."

Harry gave him a speculative look. "Still, you've been off. Your head isn't here. What gives?"

He wished he knew. Hadn't been sure what had been eating at him for a long time. All he *was* conscious of was that he *wasn't* himself, had been consumed by a restless craving for something he couldn't put his finger on.

What should have been the peak of his career, negotiating a free trade deal between his country and Mexico, a deal the critics had said couldn't be done, hadn't brought with it its usual adrenaline rush. Instead it had left him flat. Empty. Uninspired. A bit dead inside if he were to be honest.

But to try to explain that to his high-flying friends, still deeply immersed in the highs of their ultrasuccessful legal and banking careers, seemed pointless. That he, manager of a multibillion-dollar portfolio for his nation, a prince with unquestionable influence who could flick his fingers and have his heart's desire at a moment's notice, was having an identity crisis.

For what else could it be? Surely he was too young to be experiencing a *midlife* crisis?

He downed the last of his whiskey as their hostess slid off the stool beside Sofía, resisting the urge to delve too deeply into his head, because it never ended well, these ruminations of his. Thinking too much could make a man crazy.

"Maybe I need some inspiration," he murmured, getting to his feet.

"Yesss!" Harry held up a hand in victory. "I *knew* it."

Nik headed for Sofía, ignoring the group of women who had been sending unsubtle signals to their table for the past half hour. The closer he got, the more spectacular his lover became. Eschewing the rake-thin trend that always seemed de rigueur in Manhattan, Sofía had an hourglass figure that harkened back to the Hollywood starlets of the '50s and '60s. Curves that actually gave a man something to hold on to when he made love to her.

Her dark hair was up tonight, a fact that would have to change. It was the only accessory, he knew, she would need in his bed.

She was twirling a lock of her hair that had escaped her updo around a finger as he dropped down on the stool beside her, an uncharacteristically fidgety move for his ultracomposed lover. Her face was as spectacular as the rest of her as she turned to look at him: lush lips, a delicate nose and those startlingly beautiful long-lashed dark eyes.

"Your Highness," she greeted him huskily.

His mouth twisted at the game they played. "You know," he said, leaning toward her and lowering his voice, "you get punished when you call me that."

Anticipation would usually have sparked in her beautiful eyes at the exchange. Instead they darkened with an emotion he couldn't identify.

He frowned. "What's wrong? Bad sales day?"

She shook her head. "It was great. I—" She pushed her martini glass away. "Can we get out of here?"

He'd been on his way to suggesting the same thing, but there was something about her demeanor he didn't like. Those walls he'd broken down were back up.

He took out his wallet, threw some bills on the bar to cover the tab and stood up. "Meet me at the Eightieth Street entrance. Carlos will be waiting."

Sofía made a discreet exit while Nik bade good-night to his friends. A chill, at odds with the sultry heat, slid through her as she exited the building and walked toward the Bentley Carlos was pulling to a halt at the curb. He got out, greeted her by name and held the door open.

She slid into the car, its sleek leather interior filling her head with the scent of privilege and luxury. Her head swirled in a million directions as she waited for Nik. Should she tell him it was over here in the car? Short and sweet, no big scenes, which Nik would hate, then he could take her home? Or should she wait until they were at his place?

Nik joined her in the car minutes later. Instructing Carlos to take them to his penthouse on Central Park West, he lowered the privacy screen between them and the driver and sat back in his seat, his gaze scouring her face.

"What's wrong, Sofía?"

She swallowed hard. Decided the car was not where she wanted this discussion to take place. "Can it wait until we're at the penthouse?"

He inclined his head. *"Kala."* Fine.

She breathed an inward sigh of relief and sat back against the seat. Nik sank his hands into her waist, dragged her onto his lap and captured her jaw in his fingers. "You haven't properly said hello."

A wave of heat blanketed her. "We're in the car…"

"It's never bothered you before. " He lowered his head, his firm beautiful mouth brushing against hers. "And it's only a kiss."

And yet a kiss from Nik could be disastrous. Her lashes lowered as he captured her mouth in the most persuasive of caresses. Gentle, insistent, he claimed her again and again until her traitorous body responded, lighting up for him as it always did. Her lips clung to his, seeking closer contact.

Gathering her to him, Nik deepened the kiss, his fingers at her jaw holding her captive as he explored the softness of her lips, the recesses of her mouth. *All of her.*

A soft sound left her throat, her fingers curling in the thick hair at the base of his neck. Nik lifted his mouth from hers, a satisfied glitter in his eyes. "Now you don't look like a cardboard cutout. You look insanely beautiful tonight, Sofía."

"Efharisto." Thank you. A word he had taught her in his language. "And you," she murmured, "had your usual throng of fans."

His eyes glittered. "Jealous? Is that what has you off center for once? If so, I like it."

The taunt knocked some common sense into her head. She pushed a hand against his chest and forced him to let her go. Sliding off his lap, she took her seat back and straightened her hair. Searched desperately for a source of innocuous conversation to fill the space.

"Congratulations on your big deal. The analysts half expected it to fall through."

He inclined his head. "I thought it might at one point. But making the impossible happen is my forte."

She smiled. *No ego there.* But why wouldn't there be? First in his class at Harvard, a genius with numbers and forging high-stakes deals, the Wizard of Wall Street as he was known, he had turned his tiny Mediterranean island of Akathinia, a glittering former colonial jewel that hosted much of the world's glitterati, into a thriving, modern economy over the past decade, his reckless, some would say suicidal, deal making paying off with deep dividends for his country. It was the envy of the Mediterranean.

She shook her head. "Your need to win is insatiable, Nik."

"Yes," he said deliberately, his gaze trained on her. "It is."

A flush heated her cheeks. He had set out to win her after her initial resistance to his invitation to dinner and succeeded. Not a fair game, really, when she'd discovered the reckless, rebel prince had far more layers than anyone thought. Brilliant and deep with a philosophical side few knew about, he was undeniably fascinating.

She leaned her head back against the seat and eyed him. "What happens when winning isn't enough anymore?"

His lashes lowered in that sleepy, half-awake big cat look he did so well, when he was anything but. "I think I'm in the process of finding that out."

She blinked. It was the first deeply personal insight he'd given her. To have it come tonight of all nights was confusing. Tangled her up in a knot.

Carlos dropped them off. They rode the elevator, reserved exclusively for the penthouses, to the fifty-seventh floor and Nik's palatial abode.

Sofía kicked off her shoes while Nik opened a bottle of Prosecco and walked through to the salon with its magnificent views of the park, the floor-to-ceiling windows encasing the luxurious space offering a bird's-eye view of the Empire State Building and the sweep of the city with its breathtaking 360-degree perspective.

A light throb pulsed at her temples as she stood in front of the windows and took in the view. Lights blazed across the smoky, steamy New York skyline, as if a million falling stars had been embraced by the sweeping skyscrapers.

Nik's spicy aftershave filled her senses just before he materialized by her side with two glasses of sparkling wine. Tipping her glass toward him in the European-style version of the toast he preferred, her eyes on his, she drank.

Finding Nik's seeking gaze far too perceptive, she looked back at the view, following a jet as it made its way across the sky, silhouetted against the skyscrapers. It reminded her of what tomorrow was. Had her wondering if that was why she had chosen tonight to end this. Because it had reminded her of her priorities.

"You're thinking about your father."

"Yes. Tomorrow is the twentieth anniversary of his death."

"Has it gotten any easier?"

Did it ever get any easier when your father's plane dropped from the air into the Atlantic Ocean because of faulty mechanics that, properly addressed, could have saved his life? When it had cost *her* the guiding force of *her* life?

"You learn to let it go," she said huskily. "Accept that things don't always make sense in life. Sometimes they just happen. If I had allowed my anger, my sadness, my bitterness at the unfairness of it all to rule me, it's I who would have lost."

"An inherently philosophical way to look at it. But you were only eight when it happened, Sofía. It must have affected you deeply."

That seemed too slight a description for what had unraveled after that phone call in the middle of the night— her mother in her grief—her childhood ripped away in the space of a few hours with one parent gone and the other so emotionally vacant she might as well have been, too.

"I have an understanding of what it's like to lose something precious." She moved her gaze back to his. "It makes you aware of how easily it can all fall apart."

"And yet sometimes it doesn't. Sometimes you go on to make something of yourself. Create and run a successful business…"

Her mouth twisted. "Which could also fall apart if the market changes."

"*Any* business could fall apart if the market changes. It's the reality of being in the game. You don't anticipate failure, you believe in your vision."

She absorbed the verbal hand slap.

"How did you fund the business?" he asked. "You never did tell me."

"The airline was at fault for my father's accident. Faulty mechanics. The settlement was held in trust for me until I turned twenty-one. I put myself through design school on a scholarship in the meantime."

"What was the ultimate intention? The business or the designing?"

"Both. My first love is designing, but I put that on hold when we started the business. We needed to get the store in the black, pay off some investments. Now I finally feel like we're getting to the point where we can hire some staff and I can work on a line for the store."

"How many years have you been open now?"

"Six."

"Six years is a long time to wait on a dream, Sofía."

Heat singed her cheeks. "These things don't happen overnight. Interviewing is time-consuming, not to mention finding someone I can trust my baby with."

"Perhaps it's *you* you don't trust." Nik's softly worded challenge brought her chin up. "When you want something badly enough, you make it happen. There are no *can'ts* in life, only barriers we create for ourselves."

"I'm getting there." She hated the defensive note in her voice. "We don't all cut a swath through our lives like you do, Nik, impervious to anything or anyone but the end goal."

His gaze sharpened on her face. "Is that how you see me?"

"Isn't it true?"

He studied her silently for a moment. She looked away, his criticisms broaching an uncomfortable truth, one she'd been avoiding examining too closely. Putting off the designing had been practicality in the beginning when establishing Carlotta and finding a steady clientele had been a matter of survival. The problem was the longer she put it off, the harder it was to pick up her sketch pad again. Doubt had crept in as to whether she had what it took.

"You know what I think?" Nik said finally. "I think you're scared. I think you talk a good game, Sofía, but you aren't nearly as tough as you make yourself out to be. I think you're scared of investing yourself in something you care so much about because there's a chance you might fail. And it's personal, isn't it, designing for you? You're putting yourself out there. What if you do and New York rejects you? What if it *all falls apart*?"

She blinked at how scarily accurate that was. "I think that's a bit of a stretch."

"I don't." He stepped closer and reached up to trace a finger down her cheek, an electric charge zigzagging its way through her. "*I know how easily it can all fall apart.* Your words, not mine."

"Philosophical musings," she denied.

His fingers dropped to her mouth, tracing the line of her bottom lip. "I think my first impression of you at that benefit that night was right. You don't fully engage with life, you hold a part of yourself back so you won't get hurt. So there's no chance it *will* fall apart. But that's a delusion you feed yourself. Nothing can prevent a tragedy or a failure or someone walking away because it isn't right. To reap the reward you have to take the risk."

She had no answer for that because she was afraid it was true. All of it. But if it was true about her, it was equally, if not more so, true about him.

"And what about you?" she countered. "You hide yourself under this smooth veneer, Nik. No one ever really gets to know the real you. What you dream of. What you hope for. Tonight, what you said about winning, about not knowing what happens when it isn't enough anymore, it was the first time you've admitted anything truly intimate about yourself to me. And soon, my time will be up, won't it? You'll decide I'm getting too close, your attention span will wane and I'll receive a very nice piece of jewelry to kiss off and fade into the sunset."

His gaze darkened. "I never promised you more, Sofía. It's the way I am. You knew that."

"Yes," she agreed. "I did. We are two birds of a feather. Unwilling or unable to be intimate with someone else. Which is why I think we should end it now while it's still good. While we still like each other. So it doesn't get drawn out and bitter. We did promise ourselves that, after all, didn't we?"

His eyes widened, then narrowed. "You arranged to meet me tonight to *end* things between us?"

She forced herself to nod. "Be honest. You were going to do it soon, weren't you? Your silence this week was your way of demonstrating to me I can't depend on you."

His mouth tightened. "I was swamped this week, Sofía. But yes, I did think we should end it soon. I was waiting for the chemistry to burn its natural course."

Which it hadn't. She had a feeling it would be a long, long time before that happened. But it was about more than that for her now, more about who Nik was and how they connected on a deeper level. She'd thought it might be more for him, too, sometimes she could swear that it was, but apparently she'd been wrong.

She lifted her chin, her chest tight. She'd wanted to be different from the rest. Realized that's what tonight had been about. Wanting him to say they *were* different. And now she knew her delusion had been complete.

Nik closed the distance between them. There was a

dark glitter of emotion in his eyes she couldn't even come close to identifying. "It was good, Sofía."

"Yes," she agreed, shocked at how steady and resolute her voice was. "We were."

His gaze held hers—probing, searching. "Is *this* how you want to end us?"

"No." She stepped closer and lifted up on tiptoe, her eyes on his as she cupped the hard line of his jaw. "I wanted to end it like this."

CHAPTER TWO

HEAT FLARED IN Nik's gaze, wiping out the cool blue perusal that was his default expression and replacing it with a banked fire she knew preceded extreme pleasure.

He kissed her then, his lips parting hers with none of his earlier gentle coaxing. This time he demanded her acquiescence, *insisted* she give in to the electricity between them, and despite her better sense, she wanted this. She had known it would end like this, known it would *have* to end like this between them because their chemistry had always been beyond compare.

She sank into the kiss, gave herself permission to taste the lush depths of his mouth. The familiar, intoxicating flavor of him, enhanced by the wine, was deadly to her senses. She slid her arms around his waist to rest against the smooth fabric of his shirt. His hand came up to cup the back of her head, every bone in her body going liquid at the sensation of being back in his arms.

He released her lips to explore the curve of her jaw with butterfly kisses. She arched her neck to give him better access, sighing as he found the ultrasensitive spot between neck and shoulder. His fingers found the zipper of her dress and pulled it down, his palms sliding beneath the fabric, the heat of his fingers on her skin a brand she craved.

She pressed closer as his hands shifted lower to shape her hips against him. The heavy, potent force of his arousal imprinted itself on her; stirred a sweet, deep ache low in her abdomen.

"Nik..."

He pulled away from her and reached up to tug his tie loose. "Take off the dress."

She eyed him. "Was that an order?"

"What do you think?"

She couldn't deny the command was a turn-on. Power and his outrageous sex appeal were a lethal combination.

Electing to acquiesce, she slipped the straps of her dress off her shoulders, letting it fall to the floor. Nik stripped the tie off and reached for the buttons of his shirt. His eyes never left hers as he worked his way methodically down the row.

She stepped out of the dress. He crooked a finger at her. "Come here."

"I like these orders." She closed the distance between them. "You do the prince thing so well."

His mouth tipped up at one corner. He closed his fingers around hers and brought them to his unbuttoned shirt. "Take the rest off."

She slid the shirt off his broad shoulders, the anticipation of exploring all that masculine power making her feel all tied up inside. Her breath jammed in her throat as she dropped the shirt to the floor. He was so beautiful: powerful biceps and forearms honed at a Manhattan gym with a world-class boxer as a sparring partner every morning, his chest a work of art with its deep ridges defining rock-hard muscle. The sexy V that forged his lower abdomen drew her eyes to the potent masculinity straining against his trousers.

The low-grade intensity of his stare as she flicked the

button of his pants open and lowered his zipper made her stomach clench. Swallowing past her fervent anticipation, she tunneled her fingers underneath the waistband of his pants, bent and pushed them off his hips to the floor. Her position kneeling before him was undeniably provocative. As if she had been summoned to satisfy the prince's desire.

She found the thick, rigid evidence of his lust for her and freed it from his close-fitting black boxers. He was silky and mind-numbingly virile as she took him in her hands and ran her fingers from the base of him to the tip.

His hands curled in her hair. "In your mouth, Sofía. Take me in your mouth."

The rasp in his voice heated her blood. He had always loved it when she did this for him. It made him crazy. Desperate. But she didn't give him what he wanted, not right away. She teased him with her tongue first, tracing the throbbing veins that etched his shaft, exploring each one until his muffled curse filled the air. Only then did she take him deep into the heat of her mouth, again and again until his fists bunched tight in her hair and his patience failed.

"Enough."

He wrapped his fingers around her wrist and pulled her to her feet. A heady satisfaction filled her as he slid an arm beneath her knees and picked her up in a thrilling display of strength and carried her through to his bedroom. Dark and masculine it was dominated by an enormous four-poster bed. She landed on the whisper-soft silk bedspread. Nik stripped off his boxers and came down beside her.

Bracing himself on an elbow, he ran a finger across her bottom lip. "I have been craving this wicked mouth for weeks. On me, under me…"

Her heart slammed into her chest. She reached for him, curving her hands around his muscular torso. He caught her mouth in a kiss that was a blatant seduction, his tongue stroking the length of hers in a long, slow caress that made her shiver. The slide of his thumbs over her nipples deepened her shudder. They were already hard from wanting him, but his expert touch brought them to a rigid tautness that made her stomach curl, her insides ache. It had been too long since she'd had him and her body was crying out for release.

He broke the kiss, reached underneath her and unhooked her bra. The heat of his gaze on her turgid flesh made her tremble. He pushed himself upright to come down over her, his palms cupping her breasts. "I have missed these, too, *glykeia mou.*"

She closed her eyes as he took a rigid peak in his mouth. His tongue and teeth worked her nipple, the hard suction he applied intensifying the sweet ache inside of her. She moaned his name as he transferred his attention to her other nipple, his thumb teasing the damp, throbbing peak he'd left behind.

It was too much. Too much.

"Nik..."

His mouth still at her breast, he nudged her legs apart and slid his palm up her thigh. She trembled at the pleasure she knew he could give her, spreading wide for him. A guttural sound of approval left him. Her flesh was moist, ready for him as he pushed her panties aside and traced the line of her most intimate part.

God. She pressed her head back against the bed as he brought his thumb to the hard nub at the center of her at the same time he slid one of his long, masculine fingers inside of her. Her body tightened around him, missing him, aching for his touch. Nik knew how to work a woman until she begged; always made sure she was never anything less than fully aroused before he took her. Made her *wild* for him.

His eyes were hot on her face now, watching her reactions, absorbing every sound of pleasure she made. Slowly, deliberately, he brought her higher, until her hips were writhing against his hand. Then he added another finger and filled her so exquisitely, her vision glazed over. Her hands clenched the silk coverlet as the pleasure built and built until she was drowning in it.

Eyes glittering, he brought his mouth down to hers, their breath mingling. "Come for me, Sofía. *Now.*"

His sexy command pushed her over the edge. The insistent caress of his thumb against her nerve endings strung tight with tension sent her spiraling into a whitehot release that curled her toes. A release only Nik could give her.

His mouth closed over hers as he kissed her through every mind-numbing second of it, murmuring his husky approval of her response against her lips. She shuddered and grasped his powerful biceps to ground herself as the aftershocks tore through her.

He lifted himself off her, ready to retrieve a condom. The magnificence of his virility in full arousal was heartstopping. *Indescribable.* "No," she said, curling her fingers around his arm, wanting, *needing* the intimacy of them together, just them, this last night. "I'm protected. You know that. Can't it just be us?"

He hesitated, his hand midway to the bedside table drawer, then he came back to her, settling his hard body between her thighs. *"Nai,"* he murmured, bringing his mouth down to hers. "I want that, too."

In bed, out of it, in the elevator to his penthouse, their lovemaking had not lacked in creativity. But tonight, he palmed her thigh and brought it around his waist in the most traditional of positions.

"So I can watch your face," he murmured, reading her expression. "I want to see you as I take you apart, Sofía."

The dark emotion in his eyes marked him angry. Angry that she was ending it, not he. He would ensure she thought of nothing but this in the future and she was sure, in turn, he would be right.

He notched himself into her slick opening and slid into her welcoming body. She gasped as he buried himself to the hilt, pressing an openmouthed kiss against her throat as he stayed motionless deep inside her. She felt him everywhere, stimulating every nerve ending, making her entire body feel alive.

He withdrew and took her again and again, the silky sensation of his body sliding against hers incredible, imprinting itself on her mind in a possession that claimed every last piece of her. She blinked, holding back the emotion storming through her. Nik brought his mouth to her ear telling her how sexy she was, how good she felt, refusing to take his own release until she came again with him.

When she cried out against his mouth and he stiffened and allowed himself to join her in a powerful orgasm that shook them both, she had never experienced anything so exquisitely intimate as the sensation of Nik joining his body with hers without reservation.

She collapsed on his chest, catching her breath as Nik smoothed a hand over her hair. Long moments passed, moments that felt suspended in time. She should go, she told herself when their breath evened out in the shadows of the silent room. Tonight was not the night to linger. Not when it felt as if Nik had taken all the control she'd walked in here with and decimated it.

She slid out of bed, found the beautiful champagne-colored dress, slipped it and her underwear on, then found her shoes in the salon. Nik followed her, watching her silently as he leaned against the wall in the entranceway, clad only in boxers. She slipped her shoes on, pulled the last of the pins from her hair, long since having lost its updo, and smoothed a hand over it.

"Regrets?" Nik asked as she came to stand in front of him.

"No." She stood on tiptoe to brush a kiss against his cheek. "No regrets."

She left before the conversation could drag on into something painful and awkward. Carlos was waiting for her downstairs, that same pleasant smile fixed on his face as had been there earlier. She slid into the back of the car, unable to summon a smile in return, and rested her head against the back of the seat as Carlos climbed in and set the car into motion.

A raw, achy feeling invaded her. She wrapped her arms around her chest to ward it off. She'd lied to Nik upstairs, perhaps to save face. Because if this was what taking risks felt like, she didn't need them in her life. She'd rather feel empty than feel any more pain.

Fully awake and unable to sleep after Sofía left, Nik pulled on shorts and a faded Harvard T-shirt and took a glass of Prosecco into the salon.

Ending things with Sofía had been the right thing to do. She had been starting to get attached. He could see the signs; they were unmistakable for a man who'd spent his life avoiding commitment. And perhaps he'd already let it go on for too long, because hadn't he always known Sofía was different from the rest of the sycophants he'd dated? Tough with a vulnerable underside... Content to keep their affair between the two of them because she didn't care about the rest.

Content to keep it uncomplicated. And yet tonight it had gotten complicated. He had hurt her.

His insides twisted. His rule never to allow a woman too close, to trust *anyone* in his position, was based on experience. He was a target for fame seekers, for those who sought to use him to further their own agendas. Charlotte, his ex-girlfriend, who'd sold her story to the tabloids and almost destroyed his family's reputation was a prime example.

Not that he put Sofía in that category. She was different. He had trusted her. He thought, perhaps, he was more angry than anything. Angry she'd broken things off first. Angry because he'd thought their relationship still had legs—the sexual part of it that is. It was the first time a woman had initiated an end to a mutually beneficial relationship. He couldn't deny it stung.

A wry smile curved his lips. Perhaps he'd had that one coming for a long time.

He pulled out his laptop, deciding to work through a few emails he'd left earlier to attend the event. His personal aide, Abram, who must have seen the light, knocked and entered from the adjoining staff quarters.

Equal parts friend, butler and highly trained fixer, Abram was sometimes dour, frequently circumspect, but *never* flustered. And yet, right now, in the heart of the Manhattan night, he looked distinctly agitated.

"What is it now?" Nik asked. "Don't tell me—King Idas has somehow managed to put my brother's nose out of joint with yet another expulsion of hot air."

Abram fixed his faded green gaze on him. The tumultuous light he saw there made his heart skip a beat.

"Crown Prince Athamos has been in an accident, Your Highness. He is dead."

The room dissolved around him. He rested a palm against the sofa, his head spinning. "An accident," he repeated. "It's not possible. I just spoke with Athamos last night."

Abram dipped his head. "I'm so sorry, sir. It happened last evening in Carnelia. It's taken time to verify the reports."

His blood turned to ice. His mind raced as he attempted to process what his aide had just told him. His brother had been raging about Akathinia's overly amorous suitor last night, its sister island Carnelia and its king, Idas, who wanted to annex Akathinia back into the Catharian Islands to which it had once belonged over a century ago. Insanity in this age of democracy, but there were enough examples around the world to put everyone on edge.

Nik had talked his brother off the ledge. *What the hell had happened after that?*

"What was he doing in Carnelia?"

"The facts are thin at the moment. There was an argument of some sort over a woman. Prince Athamos and Crown Prince Kostas of Carnelia decided to settle it with a car race through the mountains, the same route the ancient horse race used to take." His aide paused. "An onlooker said Prince Athamos took a curve too steeply. His car plunged off the cliff and into the ocean."

An argument? Over a woman? His brother was as levelheaded as Nik was passionate and reckless. And yet he had gotten into his car and raced his arch nemesis through the suicidal cliffs of Carnelia? *His enemy's domain?* A man known to have as much fire in his veins as his hotheaded, tyrannical father…

He worked to free his throat from the paralysis that claimed it. "Are they sure…?"

"That he is dead?" Abram nodded. "I'm sorry, sir. Witnesses say there is no possibility a man could have emerged alive from that drop. They are working to recover his body now."

"And Kostas," Nik grated. "He survived?"

Abram nodded. "He was a car length behind. He saw the whole thing happen."

A red rage blurred his vision, mixing with the agony that gripped his insides to form a deadly, potent storm. He got up and walked blindly to the windows, the spectacular skyline of Manhattan unfolding in front of him.

All he could see was red.

The clink of crystal sounded behind him. Abram came to stand beside him and pressed a glass of whiskey into his hand. Nik raised it to his mouth and took a long swig. When he had emptied half the glass, his aide cleared his throat. "There is more."

More? How could there be more?

"Your father took the news of the accident badly. He has suffered a severe heart attack. The doctors are holding out hope he will survive, but it's touch and go."

A complete sense of unreality enveloped him. His fingers gripped the glass tighter. "What is his condition?"

"He is in surgery now. We'll know more in a few hours."

He lifted the tumbler to his lips with a jerky movement and downed another long swallow. The fire the potent liquor lit in his insides wasn't enough to make the reality of losing both his father and his brother in one day in any way conceivable. His father was too strong, too vigorous to let such a thing fell him. It could not happen. Not when their estrangement ate at his insides like a slow-moving disease.

He flicked a look at his aide. "The jet is ready?"

Abram nodded. "Carlos is waiting downstairs to drive you to the airfield. I thought you might want to gather some things. I will stay behind and take care of the outstanding details, cancel your commitments, then join you in Akathinia."

Nik nodded. Abram melted into the shadows.

Alone at the window, Nik looked out at Manhattan sprawled in front of him, his brother's voice, crystal clear on the phone the night before, filling his head. Athamos had sounded vital, belligerent. *Alive.* Despite the different philosophical viewpoints he and his brother had held, despite the wedges that had been driven between them in the past few years as Athamos had prepared to take over from his father as king, they had loved each other deeply.

It was inconceivable he was dead.

The sense of unreality blanketing him thickened into a dark fog with only one thought breaking through. *He* was now heir to the throne. *He* would be king.

It was a role he had never expected to have, never wanted. He had been happy to allow Athamos to take the spotlight while he did his part in New York to make Akathinia the thriving, successful nation that it was. Happy to keep his distance from the wounds of the past.

But fate had other plans for him and his brother...

Sorrow and rage gripped his heart, engulfing him like the inescapable gale force winds of the *meltemia* that ravaged the Akathinian shores without warning or mercy. His hand tightened around the glass as the storm swept over him, immersing him in its turbulent fury until all he could see was red.

Abram's horrified gasp split the air. He followed his

aide's gaze down to his bleeding hand, the shattered remains of the glass strewn across the carpet. The dark splatter that seeped into the plush cream carpet seemed like the stain on his heart that would never be removed.

Nik reached his father's bedside at noon the following day. Exhausted from an overnight trip during which he hadn't slept, worry for his father consuming him, he pulled a chair up to the king's bedside in the sterilized white hospital room and closed the fingers of his unbandaged hand around his father's gnarled, wrinkled one.

The king's shock of white hair contrasted vividly with his olive skin, but his complexion was far too pale for Nik's liking.

"Pateras."

Light blue eyes, identical to his own, opened to focus on him.

"Nikandros."

He squeezed his father's hand as the king opened his mouth and then closed it. A tear escaped his father's eyes and slid down his weathered cheek. The weight of a thousand disagreements, a thousand regrets crowded Nik's heart.

He bent and pressed his lips to his father's leathery cheek. "I know."

King Gregorios shut his eyes. When he opened them again, a fierce determination burned in their depths. "Idas will never get what he wants."

An answering fury stirred to life inside of him. "He will never take Akathinia. But if he is behind Athamos's death, he will pay for it."

"It was no *accident*," his father bit out. "Idas and his son want to provoke us into a conflict so they can use it as an excuse to swallow us up to cover their own inadequacies."

He was well aware of the reason Carnelia wanted Akathinia back in the fold, but he sought to keep a rational head. "The grudge between Athamos and Kostas has been going on for years. We need the facts."

The king's mouth curled. "Kostas is his father's errand boy."

Nik raked a hand through his hair. "The Carnelian military is twice the size of ours. Akathinia is prospering, but we cannot match what they have built up, even to defend ourselves."

His father nodded. "We have made an economic alliance with the Agiero family to acquire the resources we need. Athamos was to marry the Countess of Agiero to tie the two families together. The announcement was imminent."

His head reeled. A marriage had been in the works while Athamos had been carrying on an affair with another woman? Why had his brother not mentioned it to him?

His father fixed his steely blue gaze on him. "I will never rule again. You will marry the countess once you are coronated king. Cement the alliance."

He swallowed hard, all of it too much to process. His father's gaze sharpened on his face. "You must be a leader now, Nikandros. As strong as your brother was. The time has come to step up to your responsibilities."

His responsibilities? Hadn't he been bankrolling this nation with his work in New York? Hadn't he made Akathinia the talk of the Mediterranean—the place to visit—where almost every one of his people had a job? Antagonism heated his skin. What had it taken, five, six sentences for his father to start drawing comparisons between him and his brother? *Unfavorable* comparisons.

His father and Athamos had always been in lockstep,

their philosophies on life and ruling at polar opposites of his own. He was progressive, rooted in his experiences abroad; they remained stuck in the past, preferring to cling to outdated tradition.

He had always been the afterthought. The prince embedded in New York, quietly building the fortunes of his country while his father and brother took the credit.

His desire to make peace with his father faded on a surge of antagonism. Always it was like this.

The machine at the side of the bed started beeping. Nik lifted a wary eye to it. "You must rest," he told his father. "You are weak. You need to recuperate."

His father sank back against the pillows and closed his eyes. Nik released his hand and stood up. To battle the enemy was one thing. Locking horns with his father another campaign entirely. The latter could prove to be a far more stubborn, drawn-out war of wills.

CHAPTER THREE

SOFÍA WAS CONSCIOUS of the fact that chocolate was emotional gratification of the highest level, emotional gratification that would dissipate as rapidly as it left her bloodstream. But since nothing else was working, she was giving it her best shot.

In the weeks following her final assignation with Nik she'd promised herself she would move on. She'd been fairly successful at it, throwing herself into her work at the boutique and interviewing for a new staff member—what she considered the silver lining of her and Nik's split—the knowledge that she did, indeed, need to pursue her dream, *now* not later. But somehow, after all their weeks of keeping their relationship out of the public eye, a photographer had documented her and Nik's departure from Natalia's benefit. Had immortalized their final adieu.

Putting the whole thing behind her had become an exercise in futility. Which would all have been bad enough, if the rumors of Nik's pending engagement to the Countess of Agiero hadn't added fuel to the fire. The press were having a field day comparing her to the stately countess. If she heard herself described as the fiery temptress of Latin descent versus the icy, cool aristocrat Nik was about to marry one more time, she was going to start living up to her nickname.

Tearing the paper off the bar of dark European chocolate she'd purchased at the corner store, she shoved a piece in her mouth and began the walk back to the boutique.

She was also hurt, she acknowledged. That Nik was to be engaged to a woman weeks after their own affair had ended stung. That she was just *that* forgettable. Her rational brain told her there were political factors behind it given the countess's powerful family, but Vittoria Agiero's stunning beauty was a kick in the ribs. As was the fact she was a blue-blooded aristocrat whom Sofía would be more likely to dress than ever rub elbows with.

She tore off another piece of chocolate and popped it in her mouth. Emotional gratification had never tasted so good. Not when her mixed cauldron of emotions also included her sorrow for Nik. Her heart went out to him for what he was going through. She wanted to be there to comfort him in the storm he was facing. And how crazy was that, because he'd made it clear he didn't want her.

Still, it made her heart ache to look at the photos from his brother's funeral, from his coronation day, which had taken place a month after Athamos's death. He had looked stone-faced through all of it, devoid of emotion. But she knew it was all a cover for a man who carried his feelings bottled up inside of him.

Katharine gave the chocolate bar in her hand a wry look as Sofía made her way through the chime-enabled doors of the boutique.

"That's one a day this week. You going to let him ruin your figure along with everything else?"

Sofía scowled at the woman who'd been her best friend since design school. "This has nothing to do with him. I was too hungry to wait for lunch."

Katharine hung the dress she was holding on a hanger.

"I think you have depression hunger. The *to hell with it* kind."

"I'm also starving." Sofía set the chocolate bar down on the counter and reached for the bottle of water she'd stashed behind the register. "Like nauseous hungry if I don't eat lately. It must be the exercise."

She'd been sweating it out in a fitness class every night to take the place of her dates with Nik. It was definitely helping her figure, despite the chocolate.

Katharine gave her a funny look. "You know what that sounds like, right?"

Sofía blinked. Blanched. "*Oh, no.* It couldn't be. We were always careful. *Obsessively* careful."

Katharine shrugged. "I've just never seen you eat junk food."

A customer popped out of the fitting room at the back of the store. Her partner went to assist her. Sofía put the bottle down on the counter, a jittery feeling running through her. *There was no way she was pregnant.* She was on birth control.

She pulled her phone from her purse and checked the calendar. The blood drained from her face. *Dear God.* She was late. She hadn't even noticed given the insanity of her life of late.

"Back in a minute," she blurted to Katharine, grabbing her purse and hightailing it out the door. There was only one way to dispel the impossibility of what was running through her head.

At the drugstore, she snatched two pregnancy tests from the shelf, paid for them and flew back to the boutique, where she locked herself in the bathroom and administered them. Two solid blue plus signs later she stood looking at a disaster in the making.

"Sofía…" Katharine banged on the door. "Are you okay?"

"Fine."

Katharine's tone was grim. "Open up."

She opened the door. Held up the stick.

Katharine's face dropped. "Did you do more than one?"

Her head bobbed up and down.

"Okay," her friend said slowly, "This is what we're going to do. You're going to remain calm until you see your doctor. Then you can panic."

Except seeing her doctor the following morning only triple confirmed what she already knew. She was pregnant. And no amount of denial or panic was going to change it.

Nik lifted his gaze from the seemingly endless document recapping plans for the immediate expansion of the armed forces, his eyes having glazed over ten minutes ago. Undoubtedly it was a complex, tightly timed schedule on how the government should move forward, but he failed to see how it required fifty pages to bring him up to speed. He'd gotten the gist by page five.

Exhaling deeply, his gaze slid to the pile of newspapers on his desk. Admittedly, part of his distraction might have to do with the picture of Sofía on the front page of the society section of one of the New York papers, her face turned down as she left her apartment. Beautiful Sofía Trumped by a Countess Licks Her Wounds blared the headline.

Aside from being patently untrue—spirited Sofía could never be found lacking versus his chilly soon-to-be fiancée—the racy headlines weren't helping his merger with the Agiero family. Although when it came to Vittoria, it was hard to tell if it was just her stiff demeanor or that her nose was, in fact, out of joint. He had dined with her three times now and was actually wondering how he was going to psyche himself up to bed her. Beautiful she might be; engaging and personable she was not.

Unfortunately, he and the countess were announcing their engagement next week and his choice of who to bed would be forever taken away from him. As it had been with everything else.

His chest tightened at the thought of what he'd had and what he'd lost. Things that would never be given back to him. His brother. His life. The world as he'd known it. It was like opening a can of worms, thinking about it. He'd tried not to.

His life had been a living hell since he'd come back to Akathinia, his father's recovery slow, his country's recovery from its crown prince's death equally lengthy and sorrow-ridden, particularly given Carnelia's failure to deliver anything other than a formally worded apology via messenger. *As if that would ever do.*

His coronation had been a blur. He was fairly sure he had processed little of it, his only focus his increasingly verbose neighbor who continued to insist Akathinia was better off back within the Catharian island fold—a desire that Nik knew was motivated by economic reasons. Carnelia's economy was struggling, had been for years, and Akathinia was prospering. It wasn't hard to put two and two together.

And, if he were to be honest, he wanted, *needed* to prove to his father and the people that he had the ability to lead this country as well or better than Athamos would have. It was something that kept him up at night.

Exhaling a long breath, he took a sip of his coffee, set

the cup down and returned his attention to the report in front of him, skipping to the conclusion. His attention was pulled away once again when Abram knocked on the door and entered.

"Sorry to interrupt, sir."

He lifted a brow.

"You asked me to keep an eye on Ms. Ramirez, given the news coverage."

His fingers dropped away from the papers. "Is she all right?"

"She's fine." Abram clasped his hands together in front of him. "There has been a development."

"Which is?"

"Ms. Ramirez is pregnant."

"Pregnant?" He repeated the word as if he couldn't possibly have heard it right.

"We had a detail on her as you requested, with so many photographers still trailing her. She purchased a pregnancy test earlier this week, then saw her doctor."

Thee mou. His brain attempted to absorb what his aide was telling him. It was *inconceivable.* They had been so careful.

A buzzing sound filled his head. "And the doctor? We know for sure it was confirmed?"

"Yes."

He got to his feet, his head spinning violently. It was impossible. *Impossible.*

He excused Abram. Paced the room and attempted to wrap his head around what he'd just been told. He was going to be a father. Sofía was carrying the heir to Akathinia. It was a disaster of incalculable proportions.

It occurred to him Sofía hadn't told him because the baby wasn't his. But as soon as the idea filled his head, he discarded it. Sofía hadn't had a lover before him for a long while. *They* had been exclusive. That he knew.

So why not tell him? What was she waiting for? An image of that last time they'd been together filled his head. Woke up old demons. Sofía running a finger down his cheek. *I wanted to end it like this.* The emotion he'd read in her eyes that said she'd gotten too attached. How she'd stopped him when he'd reached for a condom… *Can it be just us tonight?*

Blood pounded his temples. Had she bedded him that night with the intention of getting pregnant? It seemed so at odds with Sofía's independent personality. With her acceptance of the no commitment rules of their relationship. Yet didn't he know from personal experience just how far a woman was willing to go to keep a prince? To preserve a relationship she knew was ending?

His head was in only a slightly better state when he found his father taking a mandated walk in the formal gardens. He curtly broke the news, without preamble. The king's leathery old face turned thunderous.

"*Pregnant? Thee mou*, Nikandros. We have all turned a blind eye to your philandering, but to have her conceive your heir? Have you lost your mind?"

His jaw hardened. "It was not planned, obviously."

"By *you*. What about by her?" He shook his head. "Has history taught you nothing?"

A red mist descended over his vision. "Sofía is not Charlotte."

"You wouldn't hear ill of your first American plaything either. Then she sold her story to the tabloids and seriously damaged the reputation of this family."

And his father would never let him forget it. Never mind the fact that Gregorios had indulged in countless affairs during his marriage, had torn this family apart and was far from a saint.

His father waved a hand at him. "No use dwelling on your irresponsibility. We are on top of this. It gives us a chance to deal with it. Consider our options."

His heart skipped a beat. "What *options* are you referring to?"

"We need this alliance with the Agieros."

What his father *didn't* say rendered him speechless. When he did recover his voice, his tone was as sharp as a blade. "This is the heir to the Akathinian throne we're talking about. What exactly are you suggesting?"

"We can make this go away. There will be other heirs."

Stars exploded in his head. He clenched his hands by his sides. "Do not utter that thought ever again."

"Don't be naive about her, Nikandros. Women are your downfall. They always have been."

Nik gave him a dismissive look. "I'm flying to New York on Friday."

His father gaped at him. "You can't leave the country right now."

"Idas is not going to start a war overnight. I'll be there and back in twenty-four hours."

"And if it gets out you've left Akathinia at this crucial time?"

"It won't."

"Send Abram."

Nik pinned his gaze on his father. "As you've just said, the country is on tenterhooks right now. I am trusting no one to deal with this extremely sensitive issue but me. I know Sofía. I know how to reason with her. We'll be back within twenty-four hours."

His father clenched his jaw. "This is insanity."

Nik shook his head. "Insanity was when Athamos

dccided to take Kostas on in a suicidal race neither of them should have survived. *This* is practicality. Sofía is carrying my heir. Marriage is the only answer."

Sofía turned the sign on the boutique door to "closed," kicked off her shoes and carried them to the register, where she started doing the nightly deposit. Working was preferable to facing up to the question of when she was going to tell Nik she was carrying the royal heir.

When she unleashed a ticking time bomb with the potential to rock a nation and its leader at a time when it needed it the least...

From the timing the doctor had given her, she had conceived her and Nik's baby the night they'd ended it. When she'd questioned the effectiveness of her birth control pills, the doctor had informed her the migraine medication she was on could have interfered with the pill's effectiveness, a fact she hadn't been aware of. A fact she'd desperately wished she'd been in possession of.

That she'd gotten pregnant that night seemed to be the only thing she *was* certain of. That and the fact that she was keeping this baby. *Treasuring* it.

Her initial shock had faded into sheer, debilitating panic as her life shifted beneath her feet once again. How could this be happening *now*, when this was her time to shine? Her time to begin her design career with her business thriving. She'd even hired someone last week to make it happen.

She knew how difficult it was to bring up a child on your own. She'd watched her mother attempt to do it after her father's death and fail under the unrelenting pressure of the responsibility. *She* had been the one to parent her mother when her mother had lapsed into a deep depression. And yet what choice did she have? Nik was marrying someone else, he hadn't wanted her and it was up to her to figure this out, regardless that the life of an entrepreneur was completely unsuitable for what she was about to take on.

Overriding it all, however, had been the elemental, protective instinct that had risen up inside of her. That had always been in her DNA. The need to treasure what she'd been given. The need to protect the fragility of life. Although the sheer, debilitating panic still came in waves, something she had to keep a handle on, using the coping techniques the doctor had given her after her father's death, lest it get out of hand. Not a place she wanted to be.

She counted the twenty-dollar bills for the third time, her concentration in tatters from all the possible scenarios running through her head. The door chimed. Katharine went to intercept the customer who'd ignored the closed sign. Sofía kept counting. Her gaze rose as a funny sound escaped her partner's mouth.

The tall, dark male standing inside the door swept both of them with an enigmatic look. "You should lock the door if you're closed. This is New York, ladies."

The deposit bag slipped from her fingers. Eyes trained on Nik, she knelt and picked it up. He walked toward her, bent and scooped up two loose twenty-dollar bills, then straightened to tower over her. Their eyes locked. Her heart jumped into her mouth. Nik in full-on intensity mode was ridiculously intimidating.

She swallowed hard. "Nik— I— What are you doing here?"

"We need to talk, Sofía."

Her mouth went dry. *He couldn't know.* She had *just* seen her doctor. Then what was he doing here when tensions were running high in his country over its aggressive neighbor? Why did he have that furious glint in his eyes?

Katharine cleared her throat. "I have plans with my sister for a drink. I'll see you tomorrow."

She wanted to beg her not to go. Would have preferred a buffer between her and Nik until she figured out how to handle his unexpected appearance. How to tell him about the baby. Instead she nodded, a sinking feeling in her stomach. She had to get it over with now. She'd already waited too long.

She forced a smile. "See you in the morning."

The store was vastly, terrifyingly quiet after Katharine left. Sofía set the deposit bag on the counter and looked up at Nik. "I'm so sorry about your brother. About everything that's happened."

He inclined his head, his abrupt nod toward the deposit bag dismissing the subject. "Finish the deposit. We'll talk afterward."

The heated expression on his face made the hairs on the back of her neck stand up. She counted the rest of the money with trembling hands and shoved it in the deposit bag. Tried to convince herself Nik was in New York on urgent business and had simply dropped in to see her.

It seemed very unlikely.

She set the deposit bag on the counter and closed the register. Nik nodded toward the bag. "We'll drop it off, then talk."

She crossed her arms over her chest. "We can talk here."

"No." He picked up her purse and handed it to her. "We'll do it at home."

She was too tired, too frazzled to argue with him. They dropped the deposit into the slot at the bank, then Nik tucked her into the back of the Bentley and slid in beside her.

She tried to ignore how much she wanted to throw up.

What he would say when she told him her news. *How* she was going to tell him.

Lost in her thoughts, vainly trying to devise a strategy, she frowned as the driver took an unfamiliar exit. "I thought we were going home."

"We are. To Akathinia."

She jackknifed into an upright position. *"What?"*

"I can't be here. The fact I left the country with Idas breathing down my neck caused my advisers considerable anxiety. We'll talk in Akathinia."

She gaped at him. "We are *not* talking in Akathinia. I have a business to run. Take me home and we'll talk there."

His gaze turned incendiary. "You lost your chance to set the rules of the game when you elected to keep your pregnancy from me, Sofía."

Dear God. He knew. She swallowed hard and forced herself to stay calm. "I was going to tell you. This week."

"This week?" He yelled the words at her, his iron control snapping. "Do you have any idea what this means?"

Her insides flip-flopped. "Of course I do. Which is why I haven't said anything yet. Because I knew you would appear just like you have now and start making decisions. And I need to understand how I feel about this first. What I want to do."

His gaze narrowed on her. "What you want *to do*?"

Heat rushed to her cheeks. "I didn't mean that. Of course I'm having this baby. It's the logistics I'm not sure of."

"Logistics we should have discussed days ago."

She stared at him. So she'd been wrong in not telling him. Did he think this was any more convenient for her with her lifestyle? Any less than a disaster than it was for him?

Her chin dipped. "We can talk about this over the phone."

He caught her jaw in his fingers, the rage burning in his eyes making her heart pound. "We aren't talking about it on the phone. Akathinian law says this child we have conceived will succeed me to the throne. It doesn't matter if he or she is born in or out of wedlock. Which means I cannot marry the countess. My alliance is dead, an alliance I needed to fund a potential war." His fingers tightened around her jaw to ensure he had her attention. "It's a huge problem, Sofía. One we need to work out *now*."

Her insides twisted. She hadn't known Akathinian law well enough to draw that conclusion. Hadn't *wanted* to know.

She took a deep breath, inhaling past the tightness in her chest. For the first time she noticed how deep the lines bracketing Nik's eyes and mouth were. How stressed he looked. This pregnancy was a disaster in the current circumstances and she had made it worse by keeping it from him.

Guilt slammed into her, swift and hard.

"Come with me," he said flatly. "Before my actions set off a national security crisis. We'll talk and figure this out."

She pursed her lips. "I would need to see if Katharine can handle the shop by herself."

"Call her."

She fished out her mobile and dialed her partner. Katharine assured her she'd be fine for a couple of days.

"All right," she said to Nik. "I'll go. We talk. And then you fly me back."

He nodded. *"Efharisto."* Thank you.

It occurred to her as they boarded the plane at a small

private airfield outside of the city that she was putting herself on Nik's turf, where he yielded complete power. The power of a king. Perhaps not the wisest of decisions, she acknowledged as the tiny jet took off and left the lights of Manhattan behind. But she couldn't add any more stress to his life. Not now.

She waited until she'd endured what was always a white-knuckle affair for her in the takeoff before curling up in one of the chairs in the seating area of the luxurious jet. Then she attacked the elephant in the room. Or aircraft, as it would be...

"I know this has huge ramifications for you, Nik, but it does for me, as well. How do we deal with the distances? How am I going to juggle a baby and the shop?"

He leveled his gaze on her. "You aren't. You're the future Queen of Akathinia, Sofía. Queens don't work."

She stared at him. *Queen?* That would entail her being married to him... "You can't be serious."

His mouth flattened, the determination on his face making her heart pound. "Unless this baby turns out to be someone else's, which I highly doubt, then yes, I am entirely serious."

She didn't like the edge to his voice or the look on his face. "Of course it's yours. How can you even ask that?"

He looked at her as if she was naive to be asking the question. "How far along are you?"

"Eight weeks."

"A blood test will confirm it, then." He lifted a brow. "Funny how we were obsessively careful not to allow a pregnancy to happen and yet, magically, it happened on that last night when you asked me not to wear a condom."

She stared at him. "*Tell me* you are not suggesting I manufactured this pregnancy."

He shrugged, his face as hard as she'd ever seen it. "It wouldn't be the first time in history it's happened."

The blood drained from her face. She yanked off her seat belt and launched herself at him, her palm arcing through the air toward his cheek. He caught her hand before it got anywhere near his face and yanked it down to her side, pulling her onto his lap.

"Bastard," she hissed at him. "I can't believe you have the nerve to say that. To *me*, Nik. *Me* of all people. I was perfectly fine with the rules. *I* ended it."

"After you *told me* how you wanted to end it." His eyes scoured her face. "Were you using a little reverse psychology on me, Sofía? Being the one to end it first so I'd realize my mistake? Then along comes a baby?"

"You are insane," she gritted out, unable to free her hands to claw his eyes out. "Have you lost your mind over the past few weeks, Nik, because clearly you know me well enough to know I would never do that."

His mouth flattened. "I *thought* I knew you. But I also know how you were acting that night. I know the signs. You were getting too attached. Women can do uncharacteristic things when they want to hang on to a relationship."

Her head felt as if it was going to explode. "I *ended* it."

"You knew I was going to."

He *was* crazy. She tugged hard on her arm but he held her tight. "I am not marrying you."

He gave her a weary look. "We will. It's the only solution."

"No, it isn't. I don't want to get married. I live in New York. I have a business there. I'm not leaving it."

"What we both *want* doesn't figure into this. The only thing that matters is that you are carrying the royal heir. End of story."

Her blood ran cold. "There are other ways to make this work."

"I'm afraid there aren't." His beautiful mouth tipped up on one side. "Think of it this way. There is now no limit to how many times we can have each other. In fact, the more the better. A spare to the throne is clearly ideal. We can work out the rest of that explosive chemistry of ours."

His hard thighs burned into her bottom. The memory of what they'd done in exactly this position in the back of the Bentley sent a heated flush to every inch of her skin. She pushed a hand against his chest. "You *have* lost your mind."

A wry smile curved his mouth. "Surprisingly, I think I've kept it over the past few weeks. And believe me, Sofía, it was no mean feat."

She stopped fighting. Her breath jammed in her lungs as her brain caught up with what was happening. "You set this up. You told me we were going to talk at home so I'd get in the car and you could get me on this plane and my will would be taken away from me."

"So smart," he mocked, lifting a hand in an indolent gesture. "And so right."

She called him the filthiest name she could think of.

His smile grew. "I'm a king, Sofía. I do what I have to do."

CHAPTER FOUR

SOFÍA PACED THE palace library, oblivious to the stunning, chandelier-accented glory of the gold-and-mahogany-hued room. She wished she knew where among the exquisite first editions and precious bound volumes she could find a thesaurus. It might help her to put a label on her current set of emotions toward Nik, because *fury* seemed too little a word.

Anger, rage, wrath—they couldn't come close to encompassing the tempestuous feelings enveloping her in waves. How *dare* Nik trick her into coming here. How *dare* he assume she would give up her life in New York and marry him, just because she was having his child. Yes, she was carrying the heir to the Akathinian throne, but *she* wasn't Akathinian. She had a business in Manhattan to run. A business that meant everything to her.

Her insides roiled, sending the heat in her cheeks even higher. And then there was the utterly inconceivable accusation he'd thrown at her. *That she'd planned the pregnancy.* That she'd wanted to *trick* him into marriage. She knew Nik was cynical in the extreme, hardened from his life in the spotlight and those who would have used him had he allowed it, but to accuse her of all people of that? It was ludicrous.

Her fury and anxiety at being so helpless, so far from

home, so *out of control* of this situation had her breath coming fast and furious. Throwing herself into one of the leather chairs near the windows, she forced herself to take deep breaths, to calm down as she watched the million-dollar yachts bobbing in the harbor.

She might not be able to change the fact that she was here, but she could tell Nik how unreasonable he was being when he returned from his meeting with the Agieros, where he was attempting to avoid a diplomatic crisis as he broke off his engagement, given the results of the blood test had proved conclusively the child she carried was his. That giving up her business, uprooting her life and moving here to a little island in the middle of the Mediterranean to become his *queen* was a crazy, untenable idea.

They would talk, she could get out of here before his mother and sister returned from a charitable engagement in Athens and all would be good.

No need to meet his family when the idea of marrying Nik was preposterous.

Nik's meeting with the Agieros did not go well. In fact, it went far worse than he'd anticipated. Clearly the family could be expected to be disappointed at the loss of the opportunity to marry into the royal family and the power and prestige that came with it, but he had not been prepared for the overt antagonism Maurizio Agiero, the head of the family, had displayed upon hearing the news Nik would wed an American and not the Countess of Agiero.

He suspected it was Maurizio's deep political ambitions that lay behind the animosity. Yes, the media was abuzz with speculation surrounding an announcement of an engagement, but Vittoria had seemed to take it in her stride, cool as usual, when he'd taken her aside to personally apologize, only raising an eyebrow when he'd referred to what was an "unexpected" turn of events.

Pulling his car to a halt in front of the white Maltese stone Akathinian royal palace that stood set back from the harbor on a rolling hill that overlooked the Ionian Sea, he handed the keys to a palace staffer, then took the steps of the wide, sweeping stairwell two by two. The Agiero alliance eliminated, there was only one other partnership that would give his family the power it needed to fund a war, and it involved his arch nemesis, Akathinian billionaire Aristos Nicolades.

His father would immediately reject the idea of an alliance with Aristos because of what the real estate developer would undoubtedly demand—a casino license for the island—but there was no alternative now. Akathinia had to protect itself.

He expected to have a fight on his hands. Fortunately for both his father's heart and Nik's exhausted body, the former king had retired early. Which meant he could attack his other pressing issue: Sofía.

He headed toward his private wing. Sofía was waiting for him in his salon, staring out the window that overlooked the gardens, the tense set of her body warning him he had a battle on his hands. She whirled around, antagonism written across her beautiful face. "You fly me here to talk and then you leave me alone all day while you go to a meeting? How is that solving our problem?"

He shrugged out of his jacket and threw it on a chair. "I apologize. My meeting took longer than I thought."

She glared at him. "I am not marrying you, Nik. You are off having all these conversations, *deciding things*, when you have no idea what I'm going to say."

He worked his fingers into the knot of his tie and

pulled it loose. "I know exactly what you're going to say. What you just did."

She blinked. "So you understand we need to negotiate how this is going to work?"

"*Negotiate* isn't the right term." He pulled the tie off and tossed it on top of his jacket. "Come to terms with our situation is more accurate."

"*I* don't have a situation. *You* do."

He started undoing the buttons of his shirt. "You are carrying the heir to the throne. You are on Akathinian soil. You most certainly do have a problem to resolve."

She stuck her hands on her hips. "You *tricked* me into coming here. This is a democratic nation. You can't hold me here against my will."

"A democratic nation in which *I* retain ultimate authority." He stripped off his shirt and dropped it to the floor. "And I seem to remember you getting on that plane of your own free will."

"Because you played on my sympathies." Her eyes narrowed as he undid the button of his pants. "What are you doing?"

"Taking a shower so we can eat." He stripped the pants off, dragging his boxers over his hips along with them. Her gaze dropped to that part of him she loved so much. "Unless you'd like to join me in the shower first?"

She shifted her attention back to his face. "No, *thank* you."

"Later then." He turned his back on her and headed for the shower. "Pour me a drink, will you? I'm tired and I'm in a filthy mood."

Later? Sofía fumed. *How about never again?* She threw a mental dagger at Nik's beautiful backside as he walked into the bathroom. He could not force her into a marriage she didn't want. She was going to say her piece and leave.

His wet hair slicked back from his face, Nik joined her on the terrace a few minutes later. In jeans and a white shirt rolled up at the sleeves he didn't do much for her equilibrium. He'd always been spectacular in a suit, but in casual clothes, he was all muscular, earthy male. Devastating.

She lifted her chin. "Why are we not having dinner with your family?"

He took a sip of the drink he'd poured himself and rested his elbows on the railing.

"I don't think you're ready for it."

Her stomach tightened. "I'm sure they must be overjoyed to have me here. Your pregnant American lover who destroyed your alliance."

His mouth thinned. "I think we should focus on the point at hand."

"I'm not marrying you, Nik. There has to be some other way to make this work. Why can't the baby stay with me in New York? We'll do regular visits back and forth, and when he or she is older, they can choose whether they want to live in New York or Akathinia."

He gave her a scathing look. "The heir to the Akathinian throne is not being raised in Manhattan. This child is a symbol of the future of the monarchy, one the people desperately need right now. Our child will grow up here. Learn the customs and intricacies of the country they will one day rule."

"But *I* don't want to live here," she argued. "I have equal say in this decision, and *I* live in New York."

"Don't be naive." His razor-sharp tone sliced over her skin like a whip. "We aren't a stockbroker and an office assistant negotiating a custody settlement. I am the King of Akathinia. And if you think I'm letting you leave this country while you're carrying my heir, you're clearly deluded. Have the baby, then leave. It's your choice. But the child remains here."

The blood drained from her face, a buzzing sound filling her head. "You aren't suggesting what I think you are."

His expression was like the Hudson on a glacially cold day. "I've told you my preference. A child needs its mother. We are good together, Sofía. We *were* good together. We can make this work."

Her heart started to race, a frozen feeling descending over her. He would take her child away from her if she didn't agree to marry him. She knew that look. Knew he was dead serious.

She pulled in a breath, but the sultry, steamy air felt too thick, too heavy to deliver the oxygen she needed. Her head whirled, the strain of the past few weeks, of wondering what she was going to do, the press invading her every quiet moment, *Nik's threats*, descending over her like a dark cloud. Inescapable. Unnavigable.

She set a palm to the railing and pulled in another breath, but it was as if the air was being sucked out of her. A layer of perspiration blanketed her brow as the dusky night spun around her. She distantly registered she was going to pass out a second before Nik's arms closed around her, catching her before she could.

He sat her down in a chair and put her head between her knees. Knelt beside her, his hand on her back, commanding her to breathe. Minutes passed before the dizziness decided which way it was going to go. Finally, her gasping pulls of air slowed to rougher, longer breaths and her head began to clear.

Nik sat her up in the chair, retrieved some water from

the dinner table and pressed the glass into her hand. "A sip," he instructed. She obeyed, hand trembling as she brought the glass to her mouth. When she'd taken a couple of swallows, she handed him back the glass. Nik set it on the table, sat down opposite her and pinned his gaze on her face.

"What was that?"

"Too much," she muttered shakily. "It's all too much." She took another deep breath. "I hardly had any lunch. I get nauseated if I go too long without eating."

He shook his head. "Unless you're an A-list Hollywood actress, that was a full-blown panic attack, Sofia."

Her mouth twisted. "Isn't that what you've already established I am?"

A glitter filled his eyes. "You know I have the patience of Jove. I will wait you out all night if I have to."

"It's everything," she said quietly. "Forcing me to come here, the plane ride, threatening to take my child away. It's too much."

He shook his head. "I'm not forcing you to stay. I'm telling you my child will remain here. The rest is up to you."

"You know that's no choice."

"Then stay. Marry me."

She gave him a frustrated look. "You don't understand what you're asking."

He studied her for a long moment. "Then tell me. Make me understand."

Her gaze dropped away from his. She had never told anyone about her panic attacks. Never told anyone what her father's death had cost her. Only Katharine and even she didn't know the depth of it. But if she was going to make Nik see reason, she had to tell him.

She fixed her gaze on him. "My father was going

on his first big business trip to London the night he died. He had worked his way up through the ranks of an investment banking firm after my parents emigrated from Chile to New York when I was two. His credentials weren't recognized the same way there as they had been back home. He had to work his way up the ladder. He'd just gotten his first promotion before the trip. He was so excited. *We* were so excited.

"I remember him telling me the night he left, before I went to bed, with this big smile on his face, 'This is just the beginning for us, *chiquita*. It's only up from here. We'll be taking trips to all sorts of exotic places.'"

A lump formed in her throat, tears scalding the backs of her eyes. She blinked them back, intent on getting through the story. "The phone call came at 3:00 a.m. from the airline. They told my mother my father's plane had gone missing somewhere over the Atlantic. That they weren't sure where it was or what had happened. My mother sat up all night waiting to hear. When she woke me up for school, I knew something was wrong. She looked like a…ghost."

She swallowed hard, but she couldn't hold the tears back. They slipped down her face like silent bandits. Nik took her hand and curled his fingers around hers. "They found the first piece of the fuselage at two o'clock in the afternoon," she continued. "My father's body was recovered the next day."

"So long," he said quietly. "That must have been torture."

Not the torture he must be feeling knowing he might never get his brother's body back… Never get that closure.

"I'm not telling you this story for your sympathy. It explains *me*, Nik. What I'm feeling. When you said that night in New York my father's death must have affected me deeply, it's hard to even describe what it did to me. I was so young. I was only eight. I didn't really understand the concept of death. I was dependent on my mother to help me understand, but she wasn't there."

He frowned. "Where *was* she?"

"Emotionally, I mean. Mentally she was…gone. My father and she, they were a team when they came to America. They'd fought so hard to make a life there. But when he died, I don't think she knew what to do. She had me…so much fear about the future. She fell into a deep depression that lasted for years. It was only because of my aunt that I wasn't taken from her."

Nik's gaze darkened. "That must have been very scary for a little girl."

She nodded. "I was lucky to have my aunt. She helped until my mother could function again. Hold down a job. But my mother was never the same. It's only recently that she's started to recover some of who she once was. She is going to marry a surgeon in the fall—a doctor who works across the street from the café where she's worked for years."

"A good ending, then."

It was so, so much more complex than that simple statement. But it was easier to nod and agree than get into it. "What I am trying to tell you is that the ground shifted beneath my feet that morning, Nik. Life as I knew it ceased to exist. Everything I thought was predictable became unpredictable. Everything that was stable was suddenly unstable. I developed severe panic attacks I had to learn how to manage. I *coped* by having to have control at all times, by being self-sufficient in every aspect of my life."

He shook his head. "That's impossible, Sofía. No one has control over their lives. We all have to work with the cards that are dealt to us." He waved a hand. "*This*, this I did not expect to happen. But it's what *is*. We all have to make sacrifices in this situation."

She thought about what he had just been through. Was still going through. "I know this is a difficult situation for you. I understand what you're saying. But my business, my life in New York is what keeps me grounded, what gives me the stability I need. I've spent the past seven years building Carlotta up. You can't ask me to throw that away."

"I'm not asking you to give it up. I will fund the business. You can hire the staff you need to help Katharine. And you can spend your free time here designing the line you've always wanted to."

"*Thousands of miles* away from my friends and family."

"They can visit. You can make regular visits to New York to check on the business."

She slid her hand out of his. She knew what it was like to grow up with only one parent, with an ever-present ache in your chest for what had been taken away from you. She would never do that to her child. But stay here with Nik, a man who didn't trust her? Who thought she'd trapped him into marriage? Was that even possible?

Nik's gaze held hers. "You of all people will be able to understand the chaos our child will undergo as heir to Akathinia. The pressure. The need for a support system. They will *need* you."

Her stomach tightened at his unfair bargaining techniques. "Always the hard-nosed negotiator, Nik. Going for the jugular."

His jaw hardened. "Our child cannot be raised anywhere but here, Sofía. You know it and I know it. The only question is what you do. What I can promise *you* is that *I* will be here for you. I will protect you. Things will not *fall apart*. We will give our child the security and stability you were left without. We will do this *together*."

A cloud of confusion descended over her. She couldn't deny this baby was bigger than the both of them. The part of her that had always trusted Nik knew he was telling her the truth, that he would protect her. But would it be enough for them to make this work?

A knock at the door signaled the arrival of their dinner. She wasn't in the least bit hungry, but Nik made her sit down and eat anyway, a few bites of each thing so she wouldn't pass out on him likely.

She'd expected him to go off and work in his office after dinner. Instead he made a few phone calls and sent a couple of emails from his laptop in the salon while she got ready for bed. Maybe he was afraid she was going to bolt and run? But where? His security would catch her before she got thirty feet from the palace.

She took a long, cool shower, thinking that might help. Standing in front of the mirror afterward, about to brush her teeth, she realized she didn't have her toothbrush. Anything to sleep in... This was *insane*.

She stalked out to the salon, a towel wrapped around her. "I have nothing to sleep in."

Nik gave her an even look. "Abram had one of the palace staff pick you up a few things. They're in the wardrobe. There are toiletries in the bathroom, as well."

She went back to the bedroom. Opened the doors of the beautifully carved antique wardrobe. Lined up beside Nik's suits were a half-dozen dresses, a couple of bathing suits and a short, sheer ivory negligee.

He had been *that* sure of her. Also seemingly assured she would grace his bed in the sexy lingerie.

She slammed the wardrobe shut. Walked out into the salon. "Give me one of your T-shirts."

He blinked. "There's something to sleep in in there, too."

"I am not here for your amusement. Give me a T-shirt, Nik."

He got to his feet, walked into the bedroom and returned with a white T-shirt.

She yanked it out of his hands, went into the bathroom and got ready for bed. She was still attempting to get to sleep when Nik joined her. She stayed on her side, curled up, wondering how one night, one decision, could so hugely impact her life. Wondering how, even now, when she hated him, she could still feel the physical pull that drew her to the man on the other side of the bed.

They had never shared a bed and not made love. It was a strange and alienating feeling that added to the fury she felt, making it impossible to quiet her head. But apparently, a self-righteous, convinced-that-he-was-right Nik wasn't having any issues sleeping. His breathing had evened out and he wasn't making a peep.

She punched down her pillow. Tucked in again. Finally admitted what she knew to be true. Her and Nik's child would be born into a firestorm. He or she *would* be a symbol of hope for a nation. As terrified as she was of what was to come, she had to forgo her own selfishness and be there for her child. So they knew they were loved. So they would carry the burden they would assume without it destroying them. It was the promise she would make to them.

Even if it meant giving up everything she knew. Even if it meant spending her days protecting her heart from Nik. Which might prove to be the biggest challenge of all.

CHAPTER FIVE

NIK WAS UP at the crack of dawn for his journey to the neighboring island of Cabeirius to meet with King Idas on neutral ground in an attempt to put an end to the tensions between the two countries. Democracy and a desire for its independence had spoken in Akathinia over a hundred years ago and it would continue to be its guiding principle.

Idas elected to be his usual provocative self in the meeting, many of his statements based on falsehoods and misleading information. Nik might have been able to counter them more effectively had his advisers been better prepared on the points in question and been able to provide him with comebacks on the fly. He had been away from Akathinian politics too long to have every fact at his disposal.

Things went from bad to worse. By the end of the meeting, he had been left flat-footed one too many times, his fury catching fire. "Your commentary is inflammatory and untrue," he bit out, slamming his coffee cup down on the table. "You are making the markets and people uneasy, Idas. Push me much further and you'll give me no choice but to shut you up."

The white-haired, craggy-faced king eyed him, his lips twisting. "So passionate, Nikandros. So unlike your brother, who listened to reason. You are living up to your reckless reputation. I wonder what will be left of Akathinia when you're done with it."

Blood pounded his head, blinding him to the room around him. He stood up, fixing his gaze on Idas. "Let me know when you are willing to act like a reasonable man."

He was still shaking with anger as the Akathinian military helicopter lifted off from Cabeirius. It wasn't until they were halfway home to Akathinia that his brain right-sided itself. He had let Idas goad him into saying things he hadn't intended to say. Into issuing threats he hadn't intended to issue. Perhaps he would have called the Carnelian king's bluff eventually, but not until he had Aristos Nicolades in his back pocket and an enhanced armed forces behind him.

It did not make his dark mood, inspired by Sofía's recalcitrance, any better, he conceded, staring out at an endless vista of blue. She had acted like a woman wronged when he'd brought her here, determined to hang on to her story that she hadn't planned her pregnancy. And although he'd been moved by the account of her father's death, by where the vulnerabilities he'd always seen in her came from, she needed to agree to this marriage. He needed this particular item off his to-do list. He had only so much head space.

Was she second-guessing her gamble of getting pregnant when it had become clear this was only a marriage of convenience for him? That he would never offer her the part of him he'd suspected she'd been beginning to want? His heart, something he wasn't sure he even had anymore.

Or maybe she'd realized just how far-reaching the consequences of her actions were and was balking at the prospect of becoming a queen?

Whatever it was, he thought grimly, it didn't matter why Sofía was acting the way she was. Dissecting her guilt wasn't his problem. What mattered was that she accept the reality of their situation before the explosive news of a royal heir got out, causing yet more uncertainty among the people. There could be no more blows to this monarchy.

Sofía stood with her hand poised on Nik's office door, a sleepless night of decision-making behind her. She knew what she had to do. *Doing it* just seemed so much harder.

She pulled in a breath, knocked as Abram had told her to, then entered on Nik's command to do so. He looked up from where he sat behind his desk, a distracted, somewhat black look on his face. When he saw it was her, he put his pen down and sat back in his chair.

"Everything all right?" she asked cautiously.

"*Kala.* Fine. Have you reached a decision?"

"Yes." She shoved her hands in the pockets of the capri pants she'd found in the closet and came to stand in front of his desk. "You were right to appeal to my past in your arguments, Nik, because you know I will never abandon my child, nor will I expose them to an overdose of the pressure you were speaking of. To that end, I want to have the final say on any choices relating to our child. I want to be a hands-on mother. I don't want nannies taking over my relationship with my child. I'll be the one to set the schedule."

"We will discuss that as required."

"No." She lifted her chin. "That is my condition for agreeing to this, Nik. As well as that I want to be able to travel frequently back to New York to check on the business as you promised. I need to be part of it."

He nodded.

"I would also like to pursue my designing, so I would appreciate it if you would find me a space in the palace to do so. A quiet space with lots of room and good light."

"Done."

"As for *us*, I will play the role of your wife as required in public, but until we learn to understand each other, there will be no intimacy between us."

"Define *understand*."

"You need to believe me when I say I didn't engineer this pregnancy. We need to have trust between us if we are going to be able to do this."

He cocked his head to one side. "How am I supposed to believe a pregnancy wasn't in your head when you suggest we forgo a condom, then all of a sudden we're pregnant?"

Heat stained her cheeks. "I don't know what possessed me to say that. I don't know, I wanted that intimacy between us. But it wasn't *planned*. The doctor is fairly sure it was my migraine medication that reduced the efficacy of the pills. I had no idea it would do such a thing."

"Right." He gave her a look as if to say he hadn't been born yesterday. Her blood boiled. "Does it really matter at this point?" he suggested harshly. "It's a foregone conclusion we're having this baby."

"Yes, it does. You want to lump me in with all the other women who have abused your trust. I won't do it, Nik."

He stared at her for a long moment. "My remaining celibate for the duration of our marriage is not an option."

"Well, then I guess we have a disagreement we have to overcome, don't we?"

"Quite." He hit the button on the intercom to call Abram in. "We can get the ball rolling on an engagement announcement, then. The sooner the better."

"What about the baby? It's too early to confirm that."

"We won't." His mouth curved in a sardonic twist. This is the time we'll use to convince the people of Akathinia their king has made a last-minute, impulsive decision to pursue his happily-ever-after. A love match. We won't confirm the baby for another few weeks, unless we have to. Abram has taken steps to ensure the confidentiality of your doctor in New York."

Her stomach dropped. He had everything figured out. He was totally in control. And where was she? Completely at his mercy. Completely at the mercy of a palace machine that would strip her life of everything she'd built as soon as this announcement went out.

From this point forward, her life was never going to be the same.

Sofía's stomach was still a mass of knots as she dressed for dinner with the royal family. An announcement of her and Nik's coming nuptials was being prepared for release the next day, along with an invitation for the toast of Akathinian society to join them to celebrate the royal engagement at a party in two weeks' time.

She had balked at the tight timeline, but calming her as he would an overexcited filly, Abram had assured it was all easily done by the palace event machine. All she had to do was be a stunning *queen-to-be*.

A thousand butterflies traced a swooping path through her insides as she smoothed the beautiful violet dress around her hips that she'd chosen from the selection in the wardrobe. The palace was flying in her favorite designer next week with a dozen dresses to choose from for the engagement party, which might seem like overkill, but when you were going to be photographed by the world, your dress pulled apart piece by piece by the fashion media, you made sure you got it right.

Her mother had sounded ecstatic when she'd called, too happy with her own engagement to pick up on the reticence in her daughter's voice. *Dreamy*, she'd called Nik. "And a prince at that, Sofía."

The fact that her mother and she were still so far apart emotionally had brought back a familiar ache. The resentment at never really having had a mother who had been there for all the big events of her life, so lost in herself as her mother had been.

How some things never changed.

Pursing her lips, she scooped her hair off her neck and twisted it atop her head rather than ruminate about things she couldn't change. Up, her hair looked elegant; down, it looked a little wild with the curls the salty Akathinian air was inspiring.

Nik appeared in the mirror behind her, sleek in a dark suit that made him look like a particularly lethal jungle cat. Her pulse sped up into an agitated, jagged rhythm as his blue gaze slid over her in a slow, thorough perusal. "Wear it down."

She pulled her gaze from him. "It channels a bit of Grace Kelly if I wear it up."

His mouth curved. "There is no Grace Kelly in you, Sofía. You are all fire with some ice thrown in to keep things interesting. Be yourself."

She reached for a clip and secured the curls into a loose chignon. Nik's eyes glittered as she turned to face him. "If I told you you look incredible in that dress," he drawled, "would you put something else on?"

"Quite possibly," she retorted. "So please refrain. We're out of time."

She went to move past him to find her shoes. Nik

caught her hand in his. A current ran through her, as if she'd curled her fingers around a dangling electrical wire, jamming her breath in her throat. *Dammit.* She had to get over this. *Him.* She *hated* him for thinking the worst of her.

He lifted his other hand, a jaw-droppingly beautiful square-cut pink sapphire held between his fingers. "This could make a nice accessory."

Her breath caught in her throat. Surrounded by a double row of tiny white diamonds, the brilliance of the light pink stone was further enhanced by pave-set diamonds that covered the entire band.

It was unbelievably beautiful. Utterly perfect.

"Do you like it?" Nik prodded.

She sank her teeth into her lip. Once, when she and Nik had been walking down Madison Avenue after dinner out, they'd passed a swish jewelry store, the appointment-only kind. She'd jokingly commented to Nik that the pink sapphire in the window could persuade her to get married someday.

He had remembered.

She stifled the desperate urge to tell him she couldn't put *that* ring on her finger and perhaps he should take it back and get another.

"You could fund the entire Akathinian army with that ring," she said huskily.

"I bought it personally. And no, I don't think it would quite do it."

He lifted her hand to slide the ring on, moving it past her knuckle to sit on her finger like a blinding pink fire.

"It's beautiful," she said woodenly. Minus the heart-felt sentiment behind it.

She pulled away from him and crossed the room to

retrieve her shoes. Nik's piercing blue gaze followed her, probing, assessing. "Are you all right?"

"Perfect." She bent to slip a shoe on.

"Greet my father first," he said. "Don't bow, he hates it, wait for him to take the lead. My mother won't wish formalities, either."

"And Stella?"

His mouth tipped up at one corner. "Stella eschews formality whenever she can get away with it."

He took her arm and escorted her down the massive circular staircase to the gold-accented foyer and through to the drawing room, where Nik's family was gathered for drinks before dinner.

Her first impression of King Gregorios as he sat in a high-back chair near the windows was of flashing blue eyes the exact light aquamarine color of Nik's, a thinning head of pure white hair and a lined face that seemed to tell the colorful story of his almost four decades of rule.

Nik placed a palm to her back and directed her to his father's chair. King Gregorios stood as his son made the introductions, his vivid blue eyes inspecting her from head to foot.

"Ms. Ramirez," the king said, inclining his head. "We had anticipated welcoming a countess to the family, but life takes unexpected turns, doesn't it?"

Stella gasped. Nik's fingers tightened against her back. "*Behave*, Father."

The heat that she was sure heightened color in her cheeks was the only indication Sofía allowed that the king's barb had landed. Queen Amara stepped forward and took Sofía's hands. She was just as elegantly beautiful as her photographs, her silver hair caught up in a knot at the back of her head, her dark brown eyes discerning beneath sharply arched brows. "Sofía," she murmured, brushing a kiss to each of her cheeks, "it is so good to meet you."

The queen pulled back, a wry twist to her mouth. "Don't mind my husband. The men in this family have a tendency to speak their minds as I'm sure you've learned from Nik."

She forced a smile to her lips. "Somewhat. It's an honor to meet you, Your Highness."

"Amara, please. You are going to be my daughter-in-law after all."

She blinked at the unreality of that. Then there was another Constantinides to meet as Stella stepped forward. More arresting than beautiful, the cool, blue-eyed blonde with those signature Constantinides eyes took her in with unabashed curiosity.

"So lovely to meet you," Stella murmured, brushing a kiss to both her cheeks. "Don't mind my father," she said under her breath as she guided Sofía toward the ornately carved bar on the other side of the room. "He is who he is."

Sofía kept her gaze firmly averted from King Gregorios. "It's so nice to meet you, too. Nik has told me how close you are."

"That I am the renegade princess, I expect?" Stella lifted a brow, eyes dancing. "And you are the scandalous American lover who destroyed an alliance. It's a match made in heaven."

She gave Nik's sister a wary look as she poured her a glass of lemonade. "If it makes you feel any better," Stella murmured, handing her the glass, "I can't stand the countess. She is a cold fish. Nik would have been miserable."

Sofía's eyes widened. She wrapped her fingers around the glass. "What is *that*?" Stella demanded, manacling her fingers around Sofía's wrist to twist it so she could see the sapphire. "I can't believe Nik broke with tradition."

"Tradition?"

"All Akathinian royal engagements are celebrated with a rare type of Tanzanian sapphire named for the Ionian Sea upon which we sit. *You* will be the first not to wear an Akathinian sapphire. Well, except for Queen Flora's daughter."

"What did she have?"

"Her eldest daughter, Terese, refused to have an Akathinian sapphire. She hadn't been married two years when she and her husband had a huge argument. Terese took the car out and got in an accident. At the time, the queen was convinced it was because of the ring. Because she'd broken tradition. She was very superstitious."

Right. Yet another strike against her and Nik.

"So the legend goes." Stella waved a hand at her. "It's foolishness. I'm so glad Nik's not the superstitious type. I'm not wearing one if I ever marry. I'm a canary diamond kind of girl."

Queen Amara strolled over to see the ring. "Nik has always been of his own mind. His coronation ceremony was very simple, bucking tradition. I hope he won't deprive us of too many traditions around your wedding. We have such lovely ones."

Nik joined them. "On that note, we're planning an engagement party rather than a garden press conference."

The queen brightened. "That's a lovely idea. When will you have it?"

"In two weeks' time."

His mother looked horrified. "Two weeks?"

"It will be good for the people. They could use something to cheer about right now."

"Yes, I expect it will. But so soon. How will we get everything done?"

"It's all in motion. You don't have to worry about a thing."

Stella clapped her hands, excitement sparkling in her eyes. "Let me help plan it. I can work with the palace staff and help Sofía with all the protocol and rigmarole."

Nik lifted a brow. "*You* teach Sofía protocol? She'll have an adviser."

Stella scowled at her brother. "I'll be the *perfect* teacher. She'll know what's old-school nonsense and what she has to pay attention to."

And with that Sofía learned that Stella always got what she wanted.

Nik was still fuming as he sat down beside his father at the dinner table in the smaller, less formal dining room. He had been inexcusably rude to his fiancée. It would not continue, but it would have to be addressed later at a more appropriate time.

His attempt to steer the conversation to innocuous ground was circumvented by the sensational news coverage of his meeting with Idas today and his father's ire. "Your stance was called aggressive," his father pointed out. "International opinion doesn't like it, Nikandros, and neither does the council."

Nik's blood boiled a degree hotter. What was wrong with his father talking politics at the dinner table? His mind hadn't been right since Athamos's death. "Idas was the inflammatory one," he said curtly. "I was merely responding to him, an error, I know. It would not have been necessary had the council representatives with me had the *facts* at hand."

"What will you do?" his mother interjected. "Idas doesn't seem to be backing down. This seems like more than rhetoric."

"I have a meeting with Aristos Nicolades tomorrow."

"Aristos?" Stella frowned. "Why are you meeting with him?"

"To discuss an economic alliance to replace the Agieros."

Nik's sister looked horrified. "But he's the *devil*."

"He is *necessary* now that Nikandros has eliminated the Agieros from the equation." King Gregorios scowled. "Now we will see the scourge of humanity his casinos will bring to Akathinia."

Nik threw his father a hard-edged look. "I don't think this is the right time or place to be discussing this. I will meet with Aristos tomorrow and we will move forward from there. Akathinia must be protected. That is the priority."

His father shook his head. "We will live to regret this. If Athamos were in charge, we would have had a deal with the Agieros. *This* would not be happening."

"Yes, well, unfortunately, Athamos was off fighting over his lover when his car plunged into the ocean and he is *dead*." All eyes flew to Nik as he trained his gaze on his father. "*I* am the one making the decisions. I say we meet with Aristos."

His father muttered something under his breath, picked up his fork and started eating. The table was so silent, the clink of the king's fork against the china was the only sound in the room.

His mother, ever the peacekeeper, asked Sofía about her dress for the engagement party. Nik mentally checked out as the conversation flowed around him, his anger too great to corral.

When coffee and dessert were offered, Sofía thankfully declined, likely no more enamored with the idea of staying at the table than he was. They said their good-nights, his fiancée promising to meet with Stella over breakfast the next morning to discuss the party.

And then, mercifully, it was over.

If the dining room had been quiet, their suite was deadly so. Nik poured a whiskey, took it out on the terrace and stood in the moonlight looking out at the gardens. The rigid set of his shoulders, his ramrod-straight spine, the explosive intensity that had wrapped itself around him all day warned her to stay away.

They didn't need any more tension between them. She should go have a bath. But her concern for him outweighed her common sense.

She slipped off her shoes and joined him on the terrace, her elbows resting on the top of the railing beside him as she considered the moon, a luminous crescent-shaped sliver that sat high in the sky.

"I'm sorry my father was so rude to you," he said. "It was unacceptable. My brother's death has hit him hard."

"You and he lock horns."

He lifted the glass in a mock salute. "A brilliant deduction."

She let that slide. "I'm sorry about the Agieros," she said quietly. "I'm sorry this is such a mess."

He flicked her a sideways glance. "What's done is done."

A wave of antagonism shot through her at the jaded glint in his eyes but she tamped it down because now was not the time. "What happened today, Nik?"

He turned to face her, a closed look on his face. "Why don't we choose another topic? This one is getting a little old."

She looked at him silently, waiting him out.

He lifted a shoulder. "He was inflammatory, as I said. Half of what he was saying wasn't true, and yet I couldn't counter it properly because my advisers didn't have the information. Weren't prepared."

"And you blew up?"

"You watched the media coverage?"

"Yes."

He looked back out at the gardens. "It was unfortunate. He pushed the right buttons."

Silence fell between them. She studied the play of the moonlight across the hard lines of his face.

"I don't think your father is the only one who hasn't processed your brother's death," she said quietly. "It's been a huge shock. You need to give yourself time, Nik. Time to grieve."

He shot her a hard look. "I don't need a counselor, Sofía."

"Well you need something. You are like a powder keg today, ready to blow at the slightest provocation."

His jaw hardened. "I'm fairly sure I've had more than my fair share of it today. It was a mistake. We all make them."

"Yes," she agreed. "We do." She laced her hands together on the railing. "Where does the antagonism between you and your father come from?"

"We've never seen eye to eye."

"And your brother and he did?"

He turned to her, his gaze firing. "I said I was *done* with this topic."

She gave him an even look. "You can dish it out but you can't take it?"

"Signomi?"

"You picked me apart that night in New York, Nik. You pointed out things about me I hadn't necessarily had the courage to address. So I could see myself clearly. Are you too afraid to do the same?"

"I see myself just fine," he growled. "I let my temper get in the way today. Forgive me if it's a bit much to have what my brother would have done thrown in my face one too many times."

She cocked her head to the side. "Did your brother's philosophies differ from yours?"

His mouth flattened. "My ideas on how to run this country, on life, are pragmatic, progressive. I have a more international view. My father and Athamos preferred to remain mired in the past. Enamored of traditions and ideals that no longer make sense. Athamos did not always recognize the need to forge his own path."

And how difficult must that have been? For his brother and father to have been on the same page and Nik on another entirely? To be on the outside of that bond?

And now, she thought, studying the deeply etched lines on his face, the dark circles beneath his eyes, him as the new king, with the weight of a nation on his shoulders, still gaining his sea legs in a role she suspected he wouldn't have chosen. A father mired in grief and of no help to him. A man in the middle of a storm.

"You called me philosophical that night in New York," she said, "about my father. I was angry, too, Nik. For a long time. I didn't understand why he was taken from me. Couldn't stop thinking *what if*. I didn't get there overnight. You won't, either."

"Your father's death was a tragic accident, Sofía. Athamos's was senseless. Selfish. He got in that car and threw his life away over a *woman*."

"And the airline could have properly serviced my father's plane. If I had carried that around with me my entire life, kept assigning blame, I would have ended up bitter and angry. Don't do that to yourself."

"This isn't the same thing."

"Why?"

"Because he played with something that wasn't his to give." His voice rose until he was nearly shouting at her. "He was the heir to the throne. He threw my country into crisis without thinking of the consequences."

"And he put you in this position."

A stillness enveloped him. The icy anger in his blue eyes morphed into a white-hot fury that made her heart race. "I do *not* begrudge the role I have been given, Sofía."

She drew in a breath, her heart pounding. "I wasn't suggesting that. I was merely saying it would be understandable for you to feel resentment for having your life turned upside down. For having all of *this* thrust upon you."

He stepped closer, the smoky scent of whiskey filling her senses as he set his glittering blue gaze on hers. "I don't *need* your understanding. What I need from you is *less complication*."

Her chin came up. "It took two of us to produce *this* particular complication."

His eyes moved over her in a hot, deliberate appraisal that melted her insides. "And it was a hell of a good time doing it, wasn't it? *That* kind of comfort I can take. Otherwise, go to bed."

Her mouth dropped open. Nails biting into her palms she stood there staring at him. He was hurting, no doubt about it. Had ghosts she'd barely scratched the surface of. But *that* wasn't going to happen.

Spinning on her heel, she stalked inside.

* * *

Nik took a deep breath and exhaled slowly, his hands gripping the railing as he leaned back and flexed his arms. Sofía telling him how to feel, how to manage the maelstrom of emotions storming his head after the day he'd just had was too much. Much too much.

You need to give yourself time to grieve. When was there time to grieve when he spent every waking hour trying to find his way out of this hell he'd been bequeathed? Of course he was angry with Athamos. *Furious* with his brother for playing not only with his own life but with his, as well. For landing him back in an arena where his father had made it clear he didn't belong. *Athamos's domain. Athamos the born diplomat.*

And maybe his father had been right. Hadn't he walked right into Idas's trap today? Done exactly what he'd expected him to? What *everyone* had expected him to—the reckless, rebel prince turned king? Proved them all right about him?

He would rectify his mistake, he knew he would. He was mostly furious with himself for allowing his emotions to get the best of him. His weakness. What his father called his Achilles' heel.

He brought the tumbler to his mouth and downed the rest of the whiskey. But it wasn't having its usual dulling effect. He was too tense, too on edge. When he was like this, when a shot of something strong couldn't block out the furor in his head there was only one thing that could relax him, and that one thing had just turned on her heel and walked away from him. Had made it clear there would be no sex until they reached an *understanding* of each other.

Well, she had that wrong. This marriage might have been thrust upon him, along with everything else he'd acquired over the past month, but he'd be damned if he was going to sacrifice the physical aspect of his relationship with Sofía when it was the part they did so spectacularly well.

He turned on his heel and strode inside. Sofía was standing in front of the mirror, brushing her hair. It fell down her back like a dark silk curtain, contrasting with her honey-colored skin bestowed upon her by her Chilean heritage.

Heat moved through him. She was so beautiful, so desirable, what she had done to him, manufacturing a pregnancy, had no impact on his lust. It only made him want to have her more.

He deposited his glass on the coffee table with a deliberate movement. Sofía's wary gaze met his in the mirror as he walked up behind her and rested his hands on her hips. "This looks fantastic on you, *glykeia mou*."

She kept the brush strokes going, rhythmically over and over. "I put the nightie on because the maid took my T-shirt. I haven't changed my mind, Nik. Get your hands off me."

"No." He lowered his mouth to her bare shoulder, scraping his teeth across her delicate skin. Her involuntary shudder made him smile. "Your body says yes."

"And I'm saying no." Her gaze speared his in the mirror. "You accused me of trapping you into marriage, Nik. You threatened to take my child away. As if you don't *know* me. Until we regain our trust in each other, this isn't happening."

Fire heated his gaze. "So you fell into the trap of wanting more. I'm past it, Sofía. I'm moving on. You should, too. Why drag this out?"

She threw the brush on the dresser and spun around. "The only thing I'm guilty of is wanting to be closer to you that night, Nik. There was no risk in my mind. If you really want me to come around, then start wrapping your head around a real relationship where we actually communicate. We're going to need it to get through this."

His gaze darkened. "And what would you like out of that *real* relationship now that you have it, Sofía? Let's get all our cards on the table. Would you like to *talk* like we did tonight? Are you looking for *love* perhaps? Or does your inability to make yourself vulnerable rule that out?"

"As much as it does for you," she bit out. "A relationship is about respecting and appreciating each other. *Knowing* each other so we can support one another. And clearly you don't know me at all right now. So we're each going to have to *learn* how to drop our guards, to let each other in, to *be* in a relationship or this isn't going to work."

His lashes lowered. "Sex is a vital part of a relationship. Sex *is* intimacy."

"It's one level of intimacy," she countered. "If I give in to you now, if I let you use sex as a weapon between us, as a way to avoid the issues we have, we are never going to confront them."

His gaze darkened. "Love is a *fantasy* people like to believe in. It has no place in the real world. We'd all be better off if we acknowledged that and viewed relationships as the mutually beneficial transactions they are."

"Transactions?" She lifted a brow. "I am certainly no expert here, given my poor track record, but my parents were in love, Nik. It was my mother's love for my father that sent her into the spiral she went into. She loved him *that* much."

"And *that* type of dependency we are to aspire to?"

"I don't know," she said. "I honestly don't know. What

I do know is that this is not working. Will not work. So figure out if you want this to succeed. And how you plan to do it."

He muttered an oath. Out of words. Out of *everything*.

She lifted her chin, her gaze on his. "What you said, in New York, about finding out what happens when winning isn't enough anymore… I think this is your chance to get to the heart of that. To confront the demons you obviously have and figure out what drives you. Otherwise, you're going to detonate like the bomb you are right now and I don't think anyone, yourself included, wants that to happen."

Turning on her heel, she stalked into the bathroom. He watched her go, clenching his hands by his sides. Why wouldn't she just admit what she'd done? Why wouldn't she just move on? He was willing to. He was being more than fair.

Diavole. He needed this thing with her sorted. *Done*. He could not fight battles on multiple fronts.

CHAPTER SIX

IN THE DAYS that followed Nik's confrontation with King
Idas, tensions continued to mount. The Carnelian king
responded to Nik's challenge to back off by mounting
a series of military exercises off the coast of Carnelia,
leaving the people of both Akathinia and Carnelia to
watch in alarm as the two countries slid closer toward
a confrontation.

It was the wake-up call Nik had needed. Sofía had
been right. His grief was ruling him. He had been allowing his emotions to dominate his thinking, gut reaction
to rule, something that might have worked in the eat-or-
be-eaten world he'd inhabited in Manhattan, but couldn't
be allowed free rein as king of his country.

It didn't matter if he hadn't wanted it, if he was still
railing against the unfairness of having his life in New
York ripped away from him, he had a nation depending
on him to make the right choices at perhaps the most
crucial period in its history. He could no longer be the
one-man show he'd been in New York where risk taking had been the oxygen he'd breathed, he had to rule by
consensus. He had to listen to *all* the voices.

He had a choice to make. He could accept the role he'd
been given and everything that came with it, *truly* accept it and move forward, or he could continue to fight

it. There was no question which way it had to go. He needed his peace of mind back.

An alliance with Aristos Nicolades in place in exchange for Nik's support of a casino license for the billionaire, Nik had come to Carnelia, his enemy's turf, to give diplomacy a shot, a council-approved plan in his hand. Although he was convinced the council was wrong in its estimation Idas was bluffing at future aggression, he would give the plan a shot, knowing a more robust armed forces was on the way as insurance.

He stood, looking out at a picture-perfect view of the mountainous Carnelian countryside, a host of emotions running through him as he waited for the king to arrive.

Athamos had perished in those mountains from which Akathinia had once been ruled, his car plunging to the rocky shore below in a death too horrific to imagine. His great-grandfather Damokles had fought for and achieved Akathinia's independence over a century ago on the Ionian Sea he could see sparkling from the king's personal salon, winning his nation's right to self-determination.

It could not be allowed to be taken away.

A door opened behind him. He swiveled to face the king, who entered the room alone. His surprise must have shown on his face for Idas shot him a pointed look, his hawkish face amused. "You came by yourself, Nikandros. I am assuming you are interested in having a frank discussion."

"Yes."

Idas waved him into a chair and sat down. "Allow me to express my condolences once again for your brother's death. It was difficult to do so with so many others in our last meeting."

Nik lifted a brow. "Kostas couldn't have said that to me personally?"

The king's eyes flickered. "My son has taken Athamos's death badly. They were rivals, yes, but their history is long, filled with a mutual respect that went very deep as you know."

"Was it a woman that provoked their disagreement?" He couldn't prevent himself from asking the question that wouldn't leave his head.

Idas shook his head. "I'm afraid I can't answer that question. Perhaps in time, we will both learn the answer."

He got the sense the old man was telling the truth. Idas rested a speculative gaze on Nik. "Congratulations on your match to the beautiful American. The star-studded engagement party is tonight, is it not? A message to the world, perhaps, Nikandros? That you have the international community behind you?"

"But we do," Nik said smoothly. "The world will not sit by and watch you do this."

The king sat back in his chair and folded his arms across his chest. "The international community seems to have a different opinion on territories with historic ties to one other. Particularly when segments of the population would prefer a return to the old boundaries. It tends to view them as local issues. Problem spots they don't want to get their hands dirty with."

"Not Akathinia. It is a former colonial jewel. Internationally loved. It would be seen as outrageous."

"Outrageous is something I'm comfortable with."

Nik's fingers bit into his thighs. "We don't need the world's help, Idas. We have the strength to make this a very bloody and costly war should you choose to take a wrong step."

"How?" the king derided. "Your military forces are nothing compared to ours."

"You have old information. Your spies should do better reconnaissance."

The king regarded him skeptically. Nik sat forward. "It's common knowledge Carnelia is struggling. Thus your need for Akathinia's rich tourism and resource base. That will never happen, but we are open to the idea of expanding trade talks with you. Lending you some of our natural resource expertise so you can further develop your own base. But this," he stressed, "is contingent on your ceasing your rhetoric in the media. On your agreement to respect Akathinia's sovereignty as we pursue discussions."

A play of emotion crossed the king's face. Greed, another hefty dose of skepticism and...*interest*. "It's an intriguing proposition."

"New sources of income are the answer, Idas." Nik drilled his point home. "Not an unpopular war."

A silence followed. "We will need some time to consider it."

"You will have it. If you give me your word you will not act militarily upon Akathinia during the time of these negotiations."

The king stood up and walked to the French doors. When he turned around after a lengthy silence, Nik knew he had won.

They shook hands. Nik walked out of the palace into the bright sunshine and on to the waiting helicopter. He wasn't stupid enough to think the threat of Idas had been neutralized. But it was a start. A very real success he could take to his critics, to the people, and move forward with.

He drew in a breath as the sleek black bird rose straight into the air. For the first time in weeks he felt as if he *could* breathe.

The palace, surrounded by the mountainous Carnelian countryside, faded to a mere blip on the ground as the helicopter rose high in the sky. He sat back in his seat and turned his thoughts to his fiancée. His other persistent problem he couldn't seem to fix. She should have been neutralized as an issue when she'd agreed to marry him. When his heir had been secured. Instead her insistence she hadn't planned her pregnancy, her demand he trust her was an impasse they couldn't seem to get past.

He agreed it was out of character for her to have done it. For the vastly independent Sofía he'd known in New York to get pregnant to keep a man. Nor was she acting like a woman who'd gotten everything she'd wanted. She was acting the opposite—as if *she* was the trapped one. Which made him wonder if it had simply been an error in judgment on her part. An impulse she regretted. Sofía reaching for the money and security she'd never had. Perhaps she hadn't even realized what she'd been doing?

Or he could be wrong. Sofía could be telling the truth. The medication may have affected the efficacy of her birth control pills. But allowing himself to believe that, that she was that honest, *different* woman he hadn't been quite ready to let go of in New York wasn't an alternative he could allow himself to consider. He wouldn't be made a fool of a second time. Not when his last mistake with a woman had produced a scandal that had rocked his family. Not when now, of all times, his head had to be clear, something it evidently hadn't been up until now.

What they needed, he decided, was a fresh start. With neither of them bearing any axes to grind. Which, he conceded, involved developing a healthy relationship between them as Sofía had said. Which he could do. He *liked* her. He admired her strength—the survivor in her. He appreciated her vulnerability—her soft underside that would make her a great mother. They had been good together in New York. If they could both move on from this, they could make a great team.

Tonight, he decided grimly, he was solving this impasse.

The helicopter banked and followed the coast, bound for Akathinia. An impulse took hold. He leaned forward and shouted an instruction to the pilot. The pilot nodded and changed direction. Fifteen minutes later, they landed on a flat patch of green halfway up the southern Carnelian mountain range.

Nik stepped out of the helicopter, walked across the field and hiked the half mile down to the treacherous, winding road that dropped away to the pounding rocks and surf below.

The site of his brother's accident was marked by the masses of flowers that lay at the side of the road, once a vibrant burst of color, now withering and dying.

Soon they would disintegrate into nothing.

For the first time since he'd been informed of the accident in that mind-numbing conversation with Abram, he acknowledged his brother wasn't coming back. Wasn't ever coming back. That this all hadn't been the horrific nightmare he'd wanted it to be. Just because they hadn't managed to find his brother's body when they'd pulled the car from the sea didn't mean he wasn't gone.

Hot tears slipped down his cheeks, scalding in the whip of the wind. *You need to give yourself permission to grieve.* He hadn't done that. Just as he'd suspected, it was a dark tunnel he had no desire to travel through.

Athamos smiling that wicked grin of his at him as they'd cut the sails in the America's Cup and declared victory for Akathinia. His brother's fierce countenance when they'd fought tooth and nail over their beliefs. His big grin when they'd made their peace with one another.

It was lost to him now. There wasn't any time left to tell him how he'd truly felt. To mend the fences that had risen between them. To ask his brother what the hell he'd been doing in that car racing Kostas that night. Answers he would never have. Answers he would have given anything to have.

In that moment, as he stared into the gray, stormy surf below, he had to believe all of this had happened for a reason. That there was some sense in this.

As the minutes ticked closer to Sofía and Nik's first official appearance together, Sofía's general demeanor vacillated from a numbness that shielded her from it all to a stubborn defiance that this media frenzy wouldn't get to her.

"It doesn't matter what I wear," she told Stella, who was putting the finishing touches on her hair. "They wanted a countess. They're going to crucify me regardless of what I show up in."

"Give them time," Stella soothed, wrapping a wayward strand of Sofía's hair into the sophisticated updo she'd engineered. "Once they get to know you, they're going to love you."

She already *had* that in New York. Her friends appreciated her. Her clients appreciated her. And yet in her first public appearance here, a visit to a youth charity with Stella, she'd been pegged as lacking in charisma. *Stiff.*

What did they expect? They had spoken of her as a foreigner from day one, incapable of understanding the nuances of Akathinian society. Nik's scandalous acquisition rumored to be pregnant. A far cry from the countess they'd been teased with, and the influence the Agieros exercised across Europe.

Was she supposed to have walked into that charity event and shone under that criticism? Under the barrage of it that seemed to come daily—when all she really wanted was to be back at the boutique, where business was booming as her face became a household name. The only upside that seemed to be coming from all this!

Stella eyed her in the mirror. "I was skeptical about you in the beginning, you know, like everyone else. Women have treated Nik as a prize to be won for so long we're all a bit jaded about it. But I can see that you care about him. That you are true, Sofía, in everything that you do. And that's exactly what Nik needs after that piece of work he was with."

Sofía frowned. "What do you mean?"

"A woman, of course. A nasty piece of work he could have done without." Stella made a face. "Rather than risk Nik's ire at divulging his secrets, I won't get into the whole sordid story. Suffice it to say he has reasons to be as cynical as he is. Give him some time, some latitude. He's worth it."

She closed her eyes as Stella engulfed her in a cloud of hair spray. If only she could confide in her future sister-in-law as to the lows her and Nik's relationship had hit. How they were hardly talking. How his mistrust of her was killing them. But as warm as her and Stella's relationship had gotten, Stella was still Nik's sister and she wasn't about to go there.

With Katharine busy running the boutique, she would have only her mother and Benetio, her fiancé, by her side tonight.

"Stop frowning," Stella murmured, fussing with one

last wayward curl. "Don't you know frown lines never go away?"

Frown lines didn't happen to be her biggest concern at the moment. Faking she and Nik were supremely happy in front of the world was. The only thing that kept her from a full-on pity party was the knowledge that Nik had placed himself on enemy territory today in an attempt to find a diplomatic solution with Carnelia. It made her stomach churn every time she thought of him meeting with that madman.

What if Idas tried something? Surely he wouldn't do anything provocative, the rational side of her brain proclaimed. The pulse pounding at the base of her neck suggested she'd be fine once he was back here all in one piece. Which was really rather traitorous behavior on her part because she *hated* him for thinking the worst of her. Hated he thought she could be so duplicitous as to trap him into marriage.

Stella made an approving sound and stepped back. "*Oriste.* You look spectacular."

"Indeed she does."

Both of them whirled around at the sound of Nik's deep, resonant voice. Sofía's pulse took off at a dead run. Not only was he in one heart-stoppingly gorgeous suit, there was a triumphant glitter in his eyes, an aura of power about him that did something crazy to her insides.

"What happened?" Stella demanded.

Nik shrugged off his jacket and tossed it on a chair. "Idas has agreed to back off while we discuss an economic renewal plan for Carnelia that Akathinia will help facilitate."

"You're kidding."

"I hope not," he said drily. "I was looking forward to giving the council some good news."

"And so you shall." Stella flew toward him and gave him a hug. "I wish I could have been a fly on the wall for that meeting."

Nik loosened his tie. "It doesn't mean the threat is gone. Idas is dangerous. But this gives us some time to build up our forces in case negotiations fall through."

Stella nodded. Glanced at her watch. "Good heavens, it's almost six. I need to get dressed."

Nik's sister whipped out of the room, promising to meet them downstairs in an hour. Sofía got to her feet, her knees a bit weak with relief. "Congratulations. I'm sure that must take a weight off your shoulders."

"For now." He crossed over to her until he stood mere inches from her. It was the closest they'd been to each other since the night of their big blowout and it set her heart thrumming in her chest. "Thank you for what you said to me that night on the terrace," he said quietly. "I needed to hear it. I needed the perspective."

Her heart skipped a beat. "If we're a team, that's what we should be doing for each other."

His gaze held hers. "Yes, we should. I want us to have a fresh start, Sofía. We need to end this impasse between us. We need to make this relationship work, for our sake and for our child's. Things may not have begun under the most ideal of circumstances, but *we* decide where our relationship goes from here. I want it to be a good one."

She pursed her lips. "But you still don't believe me about the pregnancy?"

"Sofía," he growled. "Let it go. The point is we need to move on. You said you want me to open up to you, to learn how to be in a relationship. I'm willing to do that. I'm willing to open up to you and learn to trust each other."

"To a point," she bit out. "That one thing will always

sit there between us festering." She crossed her arms over her chest and eyed him. "What's your ulterior motive here, Nik? Do you want to *fix us* so you can move on with more important things?"

His face tightened. "I'm offering an olive branch here. It would be nice if you would accept it."

"Why the sudden change in heart?"

"My parents' marriage was a political one. Amicable enough in the beginning out of the respect they had for each other. My mother came from an aristocratic family—she knew her role. But the one thing she couldn't handle were my father's affairs. Not unusual for a sovereign, but my mother has a great deal of pride. It was her one stipulation and he broke it.

"Their marriage became a war zone," he continued. "Our *home* became a war zone. I will not have that for my child. *Our* child."

"But can you trust me? *Truly* trust me?" She fixed her gaze on his. "We need that above all else if this is going to work, Nik."

His lashes lowered. "I will work on it."

Her heart dropped. She had the feeling he might never trust her. Never let go of what he thought she'd done. But what choice did she have but to try to make it work?

She spun away toward the wardrobe in search of her shoes. "You need to get ready."

"Sofía—"

"Not now, Nik." She turned around and faced him, hands on hips. "Every reporter in Akathinia is waiting for me to step into that ballroom so they can analyze me from every angle. So that they can further expose my deficiencies and label me not up to snuff. So let's just get it over with, shall we?"

His eyes widened, then narrowed. "The press will

come around. *You* need to be patient and stop worrying so much about what people think. I saw the coverage of the charity event. You didn't look like yourself at all. Stop hiding under that shell of yours and let people see *you*."

"So they can dig their claws in deeper?" She rolled her eyes. "No, thank you."

"I wouldn't do that again if I were you."

"Do what?"

"Roll your eyes."

"Why? Because you're a *king*?

"Because it's disrespectful." He stalked toward her. "What's really bothering you?"

Her chin dipped. "I just told you."

"How did the designing go today?"

"Not well. Nothing's working. I threw them all out."

He shook his head. "You can't force it. You're pushing too hard with everything. Give yourself some space. Take a day off."

"It's my sanity," she growled.

"Good thing, then, I've set aside some downtime for us."

"*Downtime?* Isn't that an oxymoron for you?"

He ignored the gibe. "Things are in control for the moment. Idas will sign. Which means you and I are going away for the weekend where we are addressing all of this, Sofía. *All of it.* I can't be fighting battles on multiple fronts."

And there was the *real* issue. Not him caring about her. She was taking up his precious brain space.

She lifted her chin. "*I* don't have time. I have a wedding to plan."

"To supervise," he corrected, stripping off his tie and starting on the buttons of his shirt. "And we aren't going far. Just to the summerhouse."

The one on the private island off the shore of Akathinia Stella had pointed out on their tour? Her stomach curled in on itself. "It's not necessary. We can work things out here."

"Like we've been doing?" He lifted a brow as he shrugged out of his shirt. "We are good together, Sofía. We will make a great team together if we can iron out this discord."

"If that's even possible."

"Oh, it's *possible*." He threw his shirt on the chair and breezed past her on his way to the bathroom. "The only variable is how long it takes for you to give in to what you know is the truth. And *how* I make you do it."

Her breath caught in her throat. "Did I actually *like* you once?"

He paused in midstride, his mouth tugging up at the corners in one of those rare devilish smiles that made her heart go pitter-patter. "You adored me once, *glykeia mou*. I'm sure you can get that loving feeling back."

"Oof." She stared at him as he walked into the bathroom. Her engagement ring shimmered in the light as she made a rude hand gesture at his back. The *cursed* ring.

"Haven't you already *doomed* us with this ring?"

He turned around, the smile fading from his face. "I bought you that ring because you loved it. Because we don't need luck. We can do this, Sofía. You just have to make the call."

She stood there, shoes in hand as he disappeared into the bathroom, the sound of the shower starting up. *Damn him.* This was not the way she needed to face the most intimidating night of her life. Off balance and suddenly unsure of *everything*.

CHAPTER SEVEN

Sofía HAD ATTENDED a seemingly endless amount of events in New York to promote her business to the fashionable women who frequented them. Hospital fund-raisers, art galas, gallery openings, society events, all at stunning venues with the crème de la crème of society in attendance. But not one of those occasions could have prepared her for the near frenetic energy that surrounded the palace as car after car of dignitaries and upper-crust Akathinians arrived under the furious shutters of the paparazzi cameras.

Lit this evening in the gold and blue national colors of Akathinia, the palace looked straight out of a fairy tale with its square turrets and gold-accented glory. Sofía and Nik stood at the center of it all at the head of the receiving line with Nik's family, Sofía in a bloodred gown by her favorite Italian designer and Nik in ceremonial military dress that made him look lethally handsome.

Her mother and her fiancé, Benetio, already inside, Sofía turned a smile on the King and Queen of Sweden, her lips feeling as if they were painted on by this point. "So lovely to meet you," she murmured to the queen.

On and on it went, for another thirty minutes, names and faces blurring into one another. Ambassadors, European royalty, upper-crust Akathinians and the filthy rich who spent their life moving from one party to the next.

She lifted her head to offer one of the final arrivals a smile. *Almost done.* And lost it immediately. Stunning in an ice-blue gown, the simplicity of which only enhanced her elegant, reed-thin figure, Sofía would have recognized the countess anywhere. She was so perfect she almost didn't look real with her coiffed, ethereal beauty.

Her own defiant choice of red suddenly screamed *overdone*.

"Countess," she murmured, inclining her head.

The countess's gaze slid over her in the same unabashed study as Sofía had given her. Sofía stood, back ramrod straight, head tossed back under the scrutiny.

"What a…sensational choice of dress," the countess finally responded, leaning forward to blow air-kisses to both of Sofía's cheeks. "It makes quite a statement. Congratulations to you and Nikandros."

Sofía drew back. *The scarlet woman*, she might as well have said. Nik's pregnant lover who'd reeled him in. She could just imagine all the labels running through the countess's head.

Frosty Maurizio and the rest of the Agieros were next, then the American ambassador to Akathinia, who, at least, finished off the endless precession on a pleasant note.

Nik curved his fingers around hers. "Now you can relax."

Relax? Was that a joke?

The paparazzi chanted their names from the bottom of the steps, the refrain growing louder with every second. Nik tugged on her hand to turn her around. "They've been patient," he said, "let's give them a good shot."

She didn't have a smile left in her as they walked down the steps toward the crowd of photographers. Not a single one. Nik slid an arm around her waist and pulled her close. "You're stiff as a board," he murmured in her ear. "You're supposed to be in love with me. Fairy-tale engagement and all that."

She pasted one last fake smile on her face. "I'm a terrible actor."

"Then don't act." He turned her toward him, his fingers curving around her jaw as he brought his mouth down on hers in a hard, possessive kiss. No avenue of escape existed with camera flashbulbs exploding all around them, Nik's less than PG-rated kiss passionate, demonstrative, demanding a response from her. Knocked completely off balance, Sofía curved her fingers around his lapel to steady herself.

The paparazzi loved it, catcalls and whistles filling the air as their flashes went mad. Sofía surrendered helplessly, for what else could she do, her lips clinging to Nik's, her body poised on tiptoe as she absorbed the magic of what it was like to be kissed by him.

A dangerous occupation.

Nik lifted his mouth from hers, eyes glittering. "Much better."

She fought for composure, heart pounding, lips stinging. "You have your reaction," she came back tartly. "We're needed inside."

His low laughter taunted her. "That wasn't even close to the reaction I'm looking for from you, Sofía. We save that for later."

Flashbulbs continued to explode in her face. She ignored him, or attempted to with her insides a hot mess of confusion.

"Sofía," a paparazzi called. "Who are you wearing?"

A genuine smile curved her lips. "Francesco Villa. He's a genius. He's making my wedding dress."

They answered a handful of other questions, then turned to make their way up the steps.

"Sofía. It's rumored you're carrying the royal heir. Care to comment?"

She froze, desperately grateful her back was to the cameras. She would have given it away in a shutter click. Nik's hand tightened around hers as they turned back to the cameras.

"I'm working on it," he drawled. "Isn't that supposed to be the enjoyable part?"

Laughter rang out. The photographer held up his camera in a wry gesture that said "I had to ask."

She and Nik resumed their path up the steps. "Better you took that one," she murmured. "Although I'm not sure that's the way I would have answered it."

They made their way into the palace and up to the second-story ballroom. The service staff scurried to ensure the guests had a glass of champagne in their hands before they made their entrance.

She stood beside Nik underneath the massive, twenty-foot-high double doors to the ballroom, her stomach spinning circles. The room looked magical cast in its blue-and-gold glow, its ten-foot-wide chandeliers dripping with crystal rivaling the jewels that adorned the exquisitely clad guests.

It was like walking into a fairy tale. *Except this was real. She was about to marry a king.*

A fleeting wish that this *was* real instead of being the pretend, practical union it was flashed through her head. She extinguished it as quickly as it came because believing in fairy tales had never been a luxury for her. That had all ended far too early in life.

A booming voice announced them. She took Nik's arm as they moved to the front of the room to give the welcome toast. The glare of the spotlight, the sensation of hundreds of eyes on her made her hand tremble as she took the glass of sparkling juice a waiter handed her. She kept her eyes on Nik to ground herself.

Nik lifted his glass. "Tonight is a joyous occasion for Akathinia. A time for us to celebrate this stunning nation we are fortunate enough to call our own, and my beautiful bride-to-be, Sofía." He turned to face her, his brilliant blue gaze resting on her face. "Sofía reminds me so much of our great country. Vibrant and proud. *Strong.* I know Akathinia will benefit from her warmth, wisdom and perspective."

Heat flooded her cheeks. It was a message, she knew, for the press and Akathinians gathered, but it did something funny to her insides.

His attention switched back to the crowd. "Let this also be a night for healing. A time for us all to move on. My brother was taken from us far too soon," he said, a rough edge inflecting his tone, "in far too unjust a way, but I know tonight, he would have wanted us to celebrate. To let him go.

"Thank you for coming," he said huskily, lifting his glass. "We look forward to sharing this special evening with you."

Sofía lifted her glass, a deep throb in her chest. It was as if he had finally let himself feel. To digest the pain that was clearly tearing him apart. She thought perhaps the message of renewal had been meant for her, too. That *they* needed to move on.

She and Nik circulated. They sought out her mother and Benetio first, who had arrived that afternoon. Sofía had never seen her mother so radiant and happy. It was bittersweet to watch with the turmoil going on inside of her. With how far apart they were emotionally. Her mother had never been able to give, only take. And yet, watching her with Benetio, their relationship looked reciprocal. Her fiancé had managed to draw her mother out of herself, something she had never been able to do.

But maybe someday that would change, she told herself, kissing Benetio on the cheek and hugging her mother. Maybe Nik was right. Maybe this was a time for renewal.

"It's all so exciting," her mother exclaimed, looking up at Sofía's fiancé. "A real king. How lucky is my daughter?"

A smile tugged at Nik's mouth. "She says that all the time. She just said it to me earlier actually. How fortunate she was to have met me."

"So true," Sofía drawled. "I could spend all day detailing your attributes. They are so...*compelling*."

Nik looked only more amused. Her mother rattled on about her own wedding plans until they were forced to move on, promising to find them later.

"Perhaps you'll catch some of your mother's enthusiasm for the wedding planning," Nik murmured as he guided her toward the next group, which he'd informed her included the devil himself, Aristos Nicolades.

"Perhaps I would," she conceded, "if I didn't have a million and one protocols to follow."

"Which are what the wedding planner is for." He pressed a palm to her back as the loosely arranged grouping that was their target parted to admit them. A tall, extremely well-built male who looked to be in his early thirties stepped forward. "Your Highness."

His designer dark stubble and piercing, black-as-sin eyes were a bit breathtaking. The dangerous, edgy vibe the stranger exuded suggested this might be Aristos Nicolades.

Nik stepped forward to shake his hand. "Aristos Nicolades, meet my fiancée, Sofía Ramirez."

Aristos's eyes moved over her in an appreciative slide that somehow managed to be proper and not so proper all at the same time. Instead of shaking the hand she offered, he brought it to his mouth, brushing a kiss across her knuckles. Nik stiffened beside her at the lapse in propriety.

"The king is a lucky man," Aristos murmured. "Congratulations."

As beautiful as he was, as fascinating as his predatory vibe undoubtedly manifested itself for just about any woman on the planet, Aristos's touch generated none of the electricity she felt when Nik put his hands on her. The magnetic realization that she had been wired for him and him alone.

The thought was more than a little disconcerting.

She retrieved her hand. "So lovely to meet you, Mr. Nicolades, after hearing so much about you."

Aristos's mouth curved. "I can imagine the king's opinion of me could prove quite fascinating. You must enlighten me."

Nik's fingers tightened around her elbow. "I am looking forward to us being on the same side, Nicolades. It should prove refreshing."

"Undoubtedly."

Nik flicked a glance over the group. "You came with someone?"

Aristos nodded toward a tall blonde immersed in conversation with another woman. "No need to introduce. It's dying a slow death."

Nik's mouth twisted. Sofía absorbed the nonchalant look on Aristos's face, then glanced over at the vivacious-looking, stunningly beautiful blonde, a response tumbling out of her mouth before she could stop it. "Does *she* know that yet?"

Aristos lifted a shoulder. "Considering the blowout we had before we came, I am fairly sure she does."

Sofía blinked. Regarded Nik's lethal rival as the two men embarked on a conversation about meeting the next week. "He's outrageous," she murmured to Nik when he wrapped the conversation and propelled her forward into the crowd. "Poor woman."

He guided her through a traffic jam. "His women are well aware of the score. I'm sure she's cognizant of the fact her expiration date is almost up."

"As was mine until the unexpected happened."

Nik leaned down and brought his mouth to her ear. "You know you and I were more complex than Aristos's careless liaisons. I hardly think they can be put in the same category."

Complex? What did that even mean? That the desire they'd had for each other had simply been more consuming than most? That it had been harder to walk away? What *would* happen when Nik's lust for her died? Would his attitude be just as apathetic and cynical as Aristos's? After all, they seemed to be two birds of a feather when it came to women despite what Nik said.

They attempted to greet everyone, but with hundreds in attendance it was almost impossible. Some of the Akathinians were gracious and welcoming to her, many more were cold and unfriendly to the outsider she clearly was. It was unnerving and depressing to put herself out there time and time again only to have her overtures thrown back in her face. By the time she and Nik moved to the center of the room to kick off the dancing, she wasn't sure if she was furious or utterly deflated.

He drew her into his arms, camera flashes extinguishing as she laced her fingers through his and set her hand on his shoulder. His gaze scoured hers. "If you let them get to you, they win."

"Easy for you to say. You haven't been the subject of a hundred snubs."

"Who cares what they think? You are *my* choice."

Because she was carrying his child. Because it was his *duty*. The humiliation that had been building inside her all evening spun itself into a fury, heating every inch of her skin. Clamping her mouth shut, she stared sightlessly over his shoulder.

"Sofía—"

"Leave it," she advised. "I'm fine."

She was anything but, but he did, likely as aware as she was that if they kept this up, the official photograph was going to be of them having a fight.

She danced with his father after that, which did nothing for her demeanor, Harry, Nik's best friend from New York, then with a succession of partners, following Akathinian tradition that the bride and groom-to-be began and ended the evening in the arms of their betrothed, but in between were encouraged to enjoy the charms of as many eligible guests as they could. To celebrate their last days of freedom as it were.

When Aristos Nicolades approached her to dance, his blonde goddess Lord knew where, she almost refused him, not sure she was up to it. Then the defiant part of her that had been kicking up its heels all evening took over.

"I would love to," she accepted, taking the hand he offered. He was wickedly tall and solid as he took her into his arms on the dance floor, moving with a smooth, commanding precision. He flirted with her with that irreverent carelessness that seemed to be so much a part of him and it was exactly what Sofía needed in her current mood. When she laughed at a particularly outrageous anecdote he recounted, Nik trained his gaze on her from across the dance floor.

Good, she thought. Let him watch.

She looked up at her dance partner. "Why don't you end it cleanly if you know your relationship is over?"

His black-as-night eyes glimmered. "Are you reprimanding me, Ms. Ramirez?"

"I think maybe I am."

He threw his head back and laughed. "Nikandros is going to have his hands full with you. No doubt about it. And yes, you are right. If I was anything but, what would the old-fashioned term be? A *cad*? I would have done so a few weeks ago."

"A woman would far more appreciate your honesty than to be treated as an expendable commodity."

An amused smile played about his lips. "Some of the women I date would prefer to bury their head in the sand when it's time to call it quits. Perhaps it is my bank account that gives them pause."

"Then you, Mr. Nicolades," she said tartly, "are dating the wrong women."

"Maybe so." He gave her a considering look. "I would wish your husband-to-be good luck taming such a fiery personality, but I have the distinct feeling he is up to the challenge. And that he will enjoy it very much."

She blushed and lifted a brow. "You think so?"

"Undoubtedly. Everyone talked about Athamos's cool negotiating skills, yet I would far rather face him across a boardroom table than Nik. Nik may be passionate, but he is the iciest, most formidable negotiator I have ever encountered when he sits down at a table. He is willing to take it to the limit, to the very edge of a deal to win. A much more worthy adversary."

Aristos's assessment of her fiancé only underscored

the sinking feeling in her stomach. She had given her life up to become queen in a country that didn't want her, for a man who thought she was a liar, who was only marrying her because she carried his heir. A man who would do what it took to have her fall in line so he could move on and rule his country. Her happiness was inconsequential.

Thinking she could ever belong to this world had been madness.

Her head reeling, a panicky feeling lingering just around the edges of her consciousness, she finished her dance with Aristos, grabbed a glass of sparkling water from a waiter's tray and sought refuge on one of the smaller, more intimate balconies, desperately needing air. Relieved to find it empty, she rested her elbows on the railing, the still warm, fragrant air drifting across her bare shoulders in a featherlight caress. It was too late to change her mind. Too late to put a halt to the chain of events she'd set in place when she'd agreed to become Nik's wife. But oh, how she wished she could in this moment. She would give anything to be back in New York, handling a busy rush at the boutique, her busy, ordinary life pulsing ahead. Instead she had descended into a version of hell she had no idea how she was going to manage.

"A bit overwhelming, is it not?"

She turned at the sound of the smooth, lightly accented voice. The countess. *Dammit*. She had done her best to avoid the woman all evening, yet here she was as if she'd specifically hunted her down.

"I needed some air," she acknowledged, turning back to look at the formal gardens, breathtaking in their color and symmetry.

The countess joined her at the railing, balancing her champagne glass on the ledge. "Akathinians are not the most welcoming to outsiders. Oh, we appreciate the influx of foreigners and the money they spend here, but when it comes down to it, they are not Akathinians. They will never achieve the same station, the same acceptance as a native with the right bloodlines."

Sofía's eyes widened. The countess held up a hand. "I'm not trying to be cruel. One could say I have, what do you Americans call it? Spoiled *grapes*? But in actuality, I'm telling you the truth. It will not be an easy ride for you."

Hot color filled Sofía's cheeks. "It seems that's the case. But since Nik has made his choice, I think the point is irrelevant, don't you?"

The countess shrugged. "Maybe so. It's unfortunate, however, that he has been forced into this course of action. It would have been easier for him to have had the Agieros on his side. A wife who understands the intricacies of what he is facing instead of one who will detract from his popularity."

Her breath caught in her throat. The countess shrugged. "The king will, at some point, realize his mistake."

"And you, Countess?" she challenged, her control rapidly dwindling. "Would you have been happy being married off for political expediency? Knowing a man was only sharing your bed because he *had* to? I would find that rather hard to swallow."

The countess's head snapped back. "It's preferable, then, to be the woman who trapped him into marriage with a baby? What else would have prompted him to break an alliance with my family?" She shook her head. "Relationships burn brightly, then they extinguish. I've had enough experience in my life to learn that. So yes, Sofía, I would have been fine with a political match. It would serve you well to lose some of your starry-eyed perspective if I can give you one piece of advice. To recognize the reality of what you are walking into."

Starry-eyed? She would have laughed at how far that was from the truth of her and Nik if it wouldn't have hurt too damn much.

Turning on her heel she stalked inside. Had she stayed she would certainly have ensured herself a position on Akathinia's persona non grata list. If she wasn't there already.

CHAPTER EIGHT

IT WAS THE early hours of the next morning before Nik and Sofía bid farewell to their final guests on the front steps of the palace. Sofía stood by Nik's side, so tightly strung underneath the hand he had placed at her waist he knew he had another battle left to fight tonight. It was in every veiled look of hostility she'd thrown at him for the past couple of hours. She'd only done it, of course, in those rare moments when it wouldn't be recorded by the cameras or hundreds of sets of eyes, but the message had come through loud and clear.

His fiancée was unhappy. Desperately so. And while he couldn't blame her given the reception the Akathinians had supplied, he had expected her to be tougher about it. Sofía had always been tough. It had been one of the things that had drawn him to her.

The senior event staffer nodded at him that they could quietly melt away. He guided Sofía into the palace and up the stairs toward their rooms. She shrugged his hand off and continued up the stairs, cheeks rosy, hair slipping from the knot atop her head, the enticing curve of her back arched above her delectable bottom as she charged on ahead of him. She was the most stunning female on the face of the planet in that moment, a curvaceous red flame any man would be wild to possess.

Including Aristos Nicolades. He had clearly been besotted with his fiancée.

Sofía threw open the doors to their suite and stalked in, headed toward the bedroom. Sitting down on the bed, she yanked her shoes off and flung them toward the closet.

Nik followed, shrugging out of his jacket and losing his tie. "So they gave you a hard ride. You knew from the press that was going to happen. We prepared you for that. Why let them get to you so?"

Her eyes darkened. "*That* was not a hard ride. That was a bloodbath. They chewed me up and spit me out, Nik. I am humiliated. No," she said, waving her hand at him, "that's not a strong enough word. I feel...*annihilated.*"

He narrowed his gaze on her. "I think you're exaggerating."

"*Exaggerating?* I made an attempt with every single one of them, *despite* their condescension. I laughed at their elitist jokes, made an attempt to *look* like I cared about cricket and the dying art of a good afternoon tea, and all I got back was a brick wall. *Nothing.* As if I might as well not even have tried. It isn't *me* that needs an attitude adjustment, it's *them.*"

"You need to calm down," he said quietly, eyeing her heaving chest. Worrying she was going to work herself into a panic attack. "Not everyone was unwelcoming. Some of the most powerful members of Akathinian society were *very* welcoming."

"I can count them on a hand." She started pulling pins out of her hair and tossing them on the bed.

"Enough of this, Sofía," he growled. "They'll get over it."

She fixed her gaze on him, twin ebony pools of fire that singed him with her contempt. "Do you know what she said to me, your countess? She told me that I will never be accepted by Akathinian society because I am just not one of you. That you should have chosen a woman who understands the intricacies of what you are facing instead of one who will detract from your popularity."

He frowned. "She said that?"

"That wasn't even the best of it. She told me it was unfortunate I wasn't taking your best interests to heart by trapping you into marriage with a baby. That you would realize your mistake of attaching yourself to a nobody like me."

He clenched his jaw. "*Thee mou*, Sofía, those are the words of a woman who has suffered her own humiliation. The Agieros have a name to protect. I don't condone her for attacking you like that, but she can be forgiven for slipping."

"*Slipping?* She came *after me*. I'd been avoiding her all evening."

That surprised him. He sighed, running a hand through his hair. "I'm sorry. I am. I wish it could have been different tonight. But it will get easier, I promise you."

She pulled the last of the pins out of her hair, the long silken tresses floating around her shoulders. Turned that volatile dark stare on him. "What do you want from me, Nik? I have agreed to this marriage. I have given up my life. And still you keep asking for more."

"I want you to stop fighting what you can't change. You're only making it more difficult for yourself."

"While you want *everything*." She glared at him, her cheeks firing a deep red. "Do you know how hard I've tried to put my past behind me? How much I'd like to forget I was the girl who lived in the apartment building none of my friends were allowed to go to because so many bad things happened there? I *had* put that behind me until the press dredged up my *meager* beginnings. Then they go and quote one of the women I *hated* from my fashion design class, who called me Scholarship Girl, who never let me forget I didn't belong in her high society circles, who refused to acknowledge the talent that got me there. Now *she*," she rasped, "was smart. She made it sound as if we were fast friends, so she could attach her name to mine for her own advantage."

He stared at her for a long moment, the misery she must have felt as a child hitting him square in the chest. He took a deep breath. "It's unfortunate, Sofía, how they have portrayed you. But if you let them destroy you over this, it's they who have the power, not you. You can't let them do that to you."

She lifted her chin. "I am *better* than that."

"Yes, you are," he agreed, sitting down on the bed beside her. "You blow me away with your strength. What it must have taken for you to survive as a young girl. So use it now. Design the best clothing line that silences them all. *Be* that designer you've always wanted to be. The people's respect will come if *you* show them who you are.

She stared mutely at him. "That's easy for you to say," she finally said. "I'm scared. I feel *lost* Nik. Hopelessly adrift. Way out of my depth. I don't know if I can do this. And that's *before* we add a child to the mix."

"Did you ever stop to think how I feel? This is new for me, too, Sofía. I am finding *my* way. Amid the press who make constant comparisons of me to my brother and father, who record my mistakes one by one. *I* have to believe in myself in this situation. Believe I can run this country, that I can set this nation on the right path. There is no room for doubt or constant second-guessing."

Her chin dipped. "Is it too much to ask for a little support along the way?"

He shook his head. "You need to do that. But you also need to tell me when you're scared. When you're feeling overwhelmed. I'm not a mind reader."

Her eyes fired. "All well and good for you to say. But since you made that promise to me a couple of weeks ago, Nik, I've seen you a total of about an hour a day, most of that time during dinner with your family. Should I book an appointment with you? Slot myself in?"

"Now you're being ridiculous."

"Am I?" She gave him a scathing look. "Aristos thought I was well in hand with you, you know. That you would enjoy *handling* me. Putting me in my place."

"You were discussing me with *Aristos*?"

"He brought it up, not me. He finds it impressive how you will take a deal to the very edge to win. Is that what you were doing earlier, Nik? *Now?* Telling me what I want to hear to solve your problem before it blows up in your face?"

"I *meant* what I said." He raked his gaze over her. "You were attracted to him."

"I wish I was. At least Aristos is an open book. What you see is what you get. God only knows with you."

Blood pounded his temples, frustration and jealousy mixing in a volatile combination. He'd had enough. *Quite enough.* He snared his fingers around her waist and dragged her onto his lap. His gaze speared hers as her lush bottom made intimate contact with his hard thighs. "You would be wise," he bit out, "to never discuss me with Aristos again. Or," he added deliberately, "to flirt with him as blatantly as you did tonight."

She didn't heed the warning. Instead her eyes went even blacker. "I thought that was the point of the Akathinian tradition… To enjoy the free members of the opposite sex before you are tied down for all eternity."

A surge of adrenaline picked him up and carried him past the point of no return. "Yes," he agreed. "It is also tradition that the bride-to-be ends up in the groom-to-be's bed. *Pleasuring him.*"

She caught her lip between her teeth. "Not this bride-to-be."

The flare of excitement in her eyes convinced him otherwise. Bending his head he tugged her lip between his teeth, taking over the job. She pushed her palms against his chest in a halfhearted shove, but her breath was coming too rapidly for him to put any stock in her protest, her luscious body in the sensational red dress plastered against him too great a temptation to resist.

His teeth sank deeper into her lip, punishing her. "You should know better than to bait me, *Sofía mou.* Or maybe that was the point?"

"As if I—" He cut off her sputter, taking her mouth in an aggressive possession designed to get to the heart of the matter. Her underneath him where she should have been for the past two weeks.

Her nails dug into his biceps in a punishment of her own. A soft sound emerged from the back of her throat, her mouth opening under his. He took advantage of it, burying his fingers in a chunk of her hair while he slid his tongue inside her mouth to taste her, stroke her. Another low moan as her fingers relinquished their death grip on his flesh reached right inside of him.

A push of his palm sent her back on the bed, her sexy red dress riding up her thighs. His hands pushed it up farther, his only intention to be inside of her. Her eyes were molten dark fire as they met his. But there was also indecision there. It made him curse low in his throat.

"There isn't one inch of you that doesn't want me to

take you right now," he rasped. "Allow us what we both want."

"I need time to think.

"About *what*?"

She pushed herself into a sitting position. "About whether I give you that power over me."

His brutally aroused body protested loudly. "I have made a promise to you, Sofía. I am committed to making this work."

"Then prove it." She shimmied to the side of the bed and slid off, the silky red dress covering up her delectable thighs. A dark brow winged upward as she turned to him. "We have all weekend, don't we?"

CHAPTER NINE

SOFÍA SPENT TWO DAYS with her mother and Benetio before they flew home to New York. They toured Akathinia, went for a cruise to the neighboring islands and spent considerable amounts of time in the jewelry shops in the Akathinian capital, where her mother fell in love with a local designer.

It was with mixed feelings that she walked her mother and Benetio down to the helicopter pad on the palace lawn for their trip to Athens. She had made an effort to connect with her mother, not an easy thing for her to ask of herself, but something in Nik's speech the night of their engagement party had resonated with her. She could either keep the shell she had built around herself intact, or put herself out there, make herself vulnerable, with the hopes of restoring her relationship with her mother. She had realized she couldn't not try.

She had told her mother about the baby. It had made her mother cry, as if breaking through some of her mother's own walls. It had been a step in the right direction for them and she'd invited her mother to come back by herself to spend some time together before the wedding.

"Thank you," her mother said, catching her up in a hug as the helicopter blades started to whir. "It's lovely to see you so happy, sweetheart." She drew back and for the first time seemed to see the conflict in her daughter's eyes. "You are happy, right? Nik is wonderful."

She bit her lip. She didn't want to worry her mother with her own wedding so close at hand. "Yes, *Mama*," she assured her, giving her mother a last tight hug. "I am happy. Call me when you're home so I know you're safe."

Her mother nodded and climbed aboard the helicopter with Benetio. It had been Nik's idea to organize the helicopter ride so the couple could enjoy the spectacular views before flying from Athens to New York. A thoughtful gesture on her fiancé's part that had Claudia Ramirez over the moon and terrified at the same time.

It seemed, Sofía thought wryly, as if her fiancé was intent on making all the Ramirez women face their fears.

Nik wrapped up his outstanding business and the next morning they flew by helicopter to the island of Evangelina, a few miles off the coast of Akathinia, to the summerhouse King Damokles had built for his wife, Evangeline. Aware of her nerves in the dipping and swaying helicopter that seemed so fragile to Sofía, Nik wrapped his fingers around hers and kept them there the entire short ride to the island.

His description of them as complex came to mind. It felt very accurate at the moment with a dozen different emotions swirling through her head. Would they be able to come to an understanding of each other? Could Nik really let her in? Trust her? Let go of his suspicions of her? Realize she was that same woman he'd met in New York? Or would their defensive barriers prove too thick for either to pierce?

Set on a pristine private island with glorious white sand beaches and surrounded by a brilliant azure sea, *summerhouse* seemed an amusing term to Sofía for the palatial villa that had been Nik's great-grandfather's hideaway, a place where he and his family could enjoy time away from the pressures of ruling.

Nik showed her around the eighteen-room villa built by a renowned Italian architect of the time, complete with fifteen bedrooms, an art gallery, a chapel and formal gardens.

"It's magnificent," she said as they finished their tour in the grand foyer with its spectacular staircase and priceless Renaissance paintings.

Nik took his sunglasses off. "It's cooling off now. I thought we might enjoy a walk and a swim before dinner."

She eyed him. "You really aren't going to work?"

"On us? Yes. On official business? No."

Her stomach rolled. The banked intensity that had swirled around her fiancé ever since she'd rejected him for the second time the night of their engagement party was an ever-present force that sat between them like a living entity. Unsure of what would happen when they unleashed the passion between them, the only thing she did know for certain was that it would change the rules of the game yet again. To what, she had no idea.

But really, she conceded, they had no choice. They had to make this work.

"I'll go change, then," she said huskily. "Will you show me to our room?"

He led her up to the ethereal, beautiful blue bedroom that overlooked a strip of white sand beach and an endless vista of blue. Dark, hand-carved furniture contrasted with the airy feel of the room, a massive canopied four-poster bed perfectly positioned to drink in the spectacular view.

A lazy morning sunrise or an evening sunset would be incredible from that vantage point, she determined, then steadfastly ignored the thought. She needed to see more evidence from Nik that he was willing to let her in before they went there.

Her clothes had been magically hung up while they had toured the villa, her bathing suits nestled in one of the ornate drawers along the wall. She slipped on a white bikini and some sunscreen, then pulled a short sundress overtop. By the time she was finished dressing, Nik had finished his call and was waiting in the bedroom for her clad only in low-slung black swim trunks.

Heavens. Her eyes drank him in. It was one thing not lusting after him when he was fully clothed, another thing entirely when so much of his tanned olive skin was on display. When the matching Vs that defined the top of his pecs and the bottom of his abs were cut deep into his rock-hard flesh in a work of perfection that begged to be drooled over. *Touched.* Paid homage to as he held himself over her and took her to heaven.

"You want to skip the walk, *glykeia mou*?" His gaze speared hers, all leashed testosterone. "I am all about a morning *nap*."

A flush heated her chest, working its way up to her face. "A walk sounds perfect." She picked up her hat and swished by him out the door. He cursed under his breath and followed. A smile curved her lips. She liked having the power for once. It was a heady feeling.

They walked along the pristine, blindingly white sand beach, cooled by a perfect light breeze that came off the sea. Nik reached for her hand and laced his fingers through hers. She didn't protest this simple intimacy because it felt so familiar, so right, it was impossible to.

She turned her gaze to the sea. It was the most perfect shade of blue she'd ever seen. Not turquoise, not the gray blue of the New York harbor, but a pure, vibrant cerulean blue that took her breath away.

Her thoughts turned to Athamos, whose body might still be out there somewhere, *was* still out there. "Do you think they'll ever find him?"

Nik looked down at her, his eyes shaded by the dark glasses he wore. "Athamos?"

"Yes."

He shook his head. "The currents are too strong. The divers spent weeks combing the waters. There was only so long we could ask them to be out there in a fruitless pursuit."

"That was the hardest part," she said. "Not ever being able to say goodbye to my father. We were fortunate they found his body. Some families were not so lucky."

He moved his gaze back to the water. "I went to the crash site after I met with Idas. It wasn't until then that I realized I was holding out some crazy hope by not finding his body with the car that perhaps it was all a big mistake, that he was alive out there somewhere. Some fisherman had picked him up, he was concussed and couldn't remember who he was. Or he'd ended up on one of the many deserted islands and we just hadn't found him yet." The grim lines around his mouth deepened. "That was, of course, wishful thinking. He would have been recognized if he was alive. And it never would have happened in the first place because no one would ever have survived that drop."

Her heart throbbing, she squeezed her fingers tight around his. "Was Idas able to shed any more light on what happened?"

"Nothing more than it was a personal dispute between the two of them. Which I believe now it was. He said that Kostas was struggling with it."

"I'm sure he must be. To be the one to survive, regardless of the dispute between them, it must be difficult."

"If guilt is *what* he is feeling, yes,"

She let that sit, the lap of the waves and the cry of the gulls the only sounds in the air.

"They had a complex relationship, Athamos and Kostas," he said after a moment. "They were rivals with a fierce respect for one other. They went to military school together. God only knows what happened between them."

She thought back to his father's cutting words that night at dinner. *If Athamos had been here, this wouldn't have happened. We would have had a deal with the Agieros.*

"Has it always been like this between you and your father? The differences you have?"

"Always."

"That must have been difficult," she said carefully, knowing she was treading dangerous waters but equally sure this was key to understanding her soon-to-be husband. "For your father and brother to be so close. For you to have such different leadership styles."

He turned his aviator sunglasses–protected gaze on her. "Confession time, Sofía?"

She lifted her chin. "I thought we were just having a conversation."

He bent, picked up a shell, examined it and tossed it back into the sea. "I have deep internal wounds because of it. It's shaped me into the closed, guarded man that I am. Is that what you want to hear me say? That my brother having my father's ear has driven a painful wedge between him and I?"

Her mouth compressed. "Only if it's the truth."

He stared at her, whatever was going on behind those dark glasses a mystery to her. "I graduated top of my class at Harvard. Summa cum laude. I was the valedictorian. And yet my father did not see fit to attend. It was not of enough importance to him. Whereas my brother's graduation from Oxford was. Where he did *not* graduate with honors. Where he was *not* valedictorian. That pretty much sums up the family dynamic."

A lump formed in her chest. "What about your mother? Are you closer to her?"

He shook his head. "My mother doesn't possess a strong maternal instinct. She left the child-rearing to our nannies. Particularly after my father's infidelities. She spent more and more time away working on her charitable endeavors."

And clearly she couldn't have divorced her husband. Leaving Nik with no anchor at home except nannies who would never be able to fully emulate a mother-son bond. It was little more than she'd had.

She frowned. "How did you handle all of that growing up? Where did you find your strength?"

"Athamos and I were close despite our differences. As were Stella and I." He lifted a shoulder. "I made my own way. Proved my worth through my own successes."

But not to his father. He could be labeled the Wizard of Wall Street ten times over and it would never attack the core of his pain.

She studied his hard, unyielding profile. Knew now that was what was at the core of Nik's demons... A father impossible to please, who had been more interested in the heir to the throne. Building success after success and never having it be enough...

"Did you want to be king? Ever, I mean?"

A frown furrowed his brow. "It was never a possibility."

"But you must have had some thoughts on the subject."

"No," he said evenly. "I didn't. I loved my life in New York. Some days I felt more American than Akathinian. It was the last thing I wanted."

"But you were restless. You needed a challenge, Nik. I'm not saying anyone would have asked for this to happen. I'm saying perhaps this happened for a reason. *You* were meant to rule Akathinia, not Athamos."

He was silent, the late-afternoon sun warming their skin as they rounded a curve and headed around the other side of the island. "I wish I'd had time to clear up some things between him and me," he said, a faraway look in his eyes. "That is my biggest regret."

Her heart contracted. "I am sure he knew. Whatever it was you needed to tell him… I felt that way about my father. I had so much I wanted him to know, but I had to believe he knew all of it. That our bond was that strong."

His inscrutable expression remained. They walked the entire circle around the island. When they returned almost an hour later, perspiration slid down Sofía's back, her skin like an oven. She stripped off her sundress, took the hand Nik offered her and waded into the stunningly warm water.

It was just cool enough to be heavenly. Slid across her senses like the most heady of caresses as they waded to deeper water and Nik drew her close. She clasped her arms around his neck, her legs around his waist, allowing him to anchor her in the bobbing waves. His eyes were an intense, brilliant blue as he held her, his palms pressed flat against her back.

"Is that open enough for you, Sofía? Have I *earned* the right to have you, then?"

Her heart tightened; poised on the edge of making a decision she knew would change everything. It *would* give him a power over her she was afraid of. And yet he was opening up to her. She had a feeling the things he'd just told her were thoughts he might not have shared with anyone else. It made her hopeful, willing to believe he was right, that they had to move on and put their trust in one other and the bond they shared. That, in time, that trust would fully repair itself.

"Was it that hard?" she asked quietly, her gaze fixed on his. "You're teaching me to take risks, Nik. That terrifies me. My *whole life* terrifies me right now."

His dark lashes lowered. "Expressing my feelings isn't easy. I wasn't brought up to do that. I was brought up to *suppress* my emotions. But I promise what I said the night of our engagement party is true. I am going to do my best to let you in."

He kissed her then. The most soulful, thorough slide of his mouth against hers. She clasped his jaw in her hands and angled her head to find a deeper contact. When it was like this, when she could feel the depth of the connection they shared, stronger than anything she'd experienced in her life, she believed they could do anything together.

They traded kiss for kiss, sensuous slides of their mouths against each other. She could have sworn the water around them heated to a higher temperature. He was hard, ready, his erection insistent against her stomach. She was putty in his hands as the sun beat down on them, her body melting into his. But he lifted his head, his lust-infused gaze tangling with hers.

"I want a bed underneath us, *kardia mou*. Do not expect to sleep."

The sun was scheduled to set just after six. Nik instructed the chef to leave dinner for them to have later, then waved the Paris-trained cook off to spend the night with her family. He did the same with the turndown staff who hovered to see to their needs.

He was craving his fiancée. He wanted no interruptions.

He waited for Sofía outside on the checkerboard marble terrace that overlooked the sea, resplendent with its stunning statues of Achilles in various poses and battles. Queen Evangeline had been a lover of Greek mythology, her obsession with the stories she'd adored apparent not only here, but in the frescos that covered the ceilings of the villa and the magnificent artwork on the walls.

The sun began its slow descent into the horizon, a golden-orange ball of fire sinking toward an endless horizon of blue. He wondered, as he drank in the spectacular sight only an Akathinian sunset could provide, about what Sofía had said earlier. About his wanting to become king. What made him so restless it was hard to be in his own skin at times…? What *drove* him?

He knew the answer lay *here*, in the heritage he had tried so ineffectively to distance himself from in New York. How every time he was in his father's presence, that interaction seemed to strip away every success he'd racked up until he was no more than the black sheep he'd always been.

Had he really loved his life in New York that much? Or had he convinced himself he didn't want to be king because that had been easier to swallow than being second best? It had been simple to tell himself his adrenaline-inducing life in Manhattan had given him the freedom and power he'd craved. Honest to a degree. He'd had the ability to determine his own destiny, what more could a man want? But now he wondered if he'd been running away from the one thing he'd needed to address. To conquer. The need to prove he was not second best. That his father had been wrong about him.

Was that why he'd felt unfulfilled in New York of late? Unsure where to go next? Because until he wrestled this particular demon to the ground he would never find peace?

He had outmaneuvered a tricky player in Idas and found a solution that benefited both countries, one which would hopefully keep his people out of a prolonged and bloody war. He had put what his father thought behind him and focused on what the country needed now. It wasn't about winning, defeating Idas, it was about *leading*.

"No thinking about work."

Sofía's husky, sensual voice slid over his senses. He turned slowly, drinking her in. Her dark wavy hair was loose around her shoulders, her olive green dress simple, her feet bare.

The connection they shared enveloped him; drew him in. He had never wanted her more.

"I wasn't thinking about work," he drawled. "I had a far more compelling subject on my mind."

She swallowed, the muscles at the base of her slim throat convulsing. He held out a hand. She walked to him and slid her palm in his. "Would you like to share?"

"I would like to *show*. But first we should drink a toast. And eat before you pass out on me."

"A toast?" she queried.

He handed her a glass of the nonalcoholic champagne he'd had chilled. "To us. To a new beginning."

She lifted her dark gaze to his and raised her glass. "To new beginnings."

They drank as they watched the sun sink into the horizon, a hazy pink lancing blue as it made its fiery descent. When it took its final dip into the ocean, bidding adieu to the spectacular show, Nik turned to Sofía. "We should eat."

She stood on tiptoe, brought her mouth to his ear and told him, very explicitly, what she *was* hungry for. And it wasn't food.

His blood fired. "You won't pass out on me?"

"Depends on what you do to me."

He picked her up in his arms and headed for the villa, his heart pounding with anticipation. Heading for the wide set of stairs, he carried her up to their room, set her down on the floor and flicked on a light.

He reached for the buttons of his shirt while Sofía walked to the window to look at the pink sky the sunset had left behind.

"I can't imagine a more spectacular view than this."

"I can," he growled, his frustration bubbling over as he ditched his shirt.

She turned, an amused smile twisting her mouth. "I've kept you waiting long enough, King Nikandros?"

He collected her from the window by way of response, picked her up and carried her to the bed. Depositing her on the silk coverlet, his hands moved to the zipper of her dress, yanking it down to expose the creamy skin he coveted.

He stripped the dress off her shoulders and pushed it down to her waist. Her breasts had swelled, bursting from the lacy cups of her bra. The blatant reminder of the child they had conceived together stopped him in his tracks. Stole his breath. The heir to this country, yes, but also *their* baby. The product of that mind-numbingly sensual night they had spent together.

He hadn't stopped long enough during the insanity of the past few weeks to even think about *this*. To come face-to-face with the evidence that he would be a father in short order was earthshakingly real. *Mind-bending.*

He splayed his fingers across her abdomen, where her flat stomach was just beginning to turn convex. "You are so beautiful," he said huskily, bending to bring his mouth to hers. "I only want you more."

He consumed her then with a kiss that plundered

every inch of her beautiful lips. She arched her neck back, giving him full access to the heat of her mouth. The sweetness he craved.

His palms cupped her engorged breasts, the skate of his thumbs across her nipples pulling a hiss from her throat.

"Sensitive?"

She nodded, ebony eyes drunk with a heavy dark desire. He bent his head and took a lace-covered nipple into his mouth, her low moan kicking him in the gut. Determined to master the insatiable urge to possess her *now* without waiting, he brushed his thumb over her other nipple as he sucked hard; laved her with his teeth and tongue until her fingers were buried in his hair, tugging. *Demanding.* He transferred his attention to her other nipple, bringing it to the same erect attention as its twin.

Sofía uttered his name on a low, sweet moan. He pulled free, surveying her complete surrender with satisfaction. "What do you want?" he asked roughly. "Tell me."

Her fingers traced a provocative path down his chest to capture his hand and bring it to her inner thigh. He closed his fingers around her soft, silky flesh. *"Tell me."*

"I want your hands on me. Here."

His inner beast liked that. A lot. Because he loved to touch her there. To feel how much she desired him. To *taste* it.

He sank his knee down on the bed between her thighs and moved his hand up, pushing her dress higher until his fingers came into contact with the edge of her silk panties. Her breath hissed through her teeth. "Here?" he asked, sliding his finger along the edge of the silk.

"Yes."

He pushed the silk aside with one hand, tracing his

thumb along her cleft with the other. She jerked against him, her highly sensitized reaction heating his blood. He dipped deeper, probing her wet, hot flesh. His sex throbbed to life at such an overt display of her desire for him.

He took her lips in an erotic, openmouthed kiss as he sank his fingers into her. He had big hands, powerful hands, and she moaned into his mouth as he filled her. He wanted her crazy, his inner beast dictated. As desperate as he'd been for her for weeks.

"Nik—please—"

He thrust his fingers deeper into her. "Tell me, *glykeia mou*."

"More," she begged. "More, please…"

He caught her lip in his teeth. "You want my mouth on you?"

"*Yes.*"

He pushed her back on the bed and dragged her dress up to her waist. The need to taste her, to claim her, swept over him in the basest of urges. Lying there, her gorgeous hair fanned out on the bed, her dark eyes hot with desire, she was everything he'd ever coveted. The only woman who could destroy his control with her exotic, sensual beauty.

"Give yourself to me," he commanded, his mouth taking hers in a hot, breathy kiss.

She knew the command, spread her legs for him in that half-uninhibited, half-shy way that made him crazy. Her eyes burned into his as he worked his way down her body, watching him the whole time. And then his brain went a hazy gray as her scent blurred the thoughts in his head until there was nothing but the soft, sweet flesh between her legs under his mouth, the rounded globes of her bottom he cupped to hold her where he wanted her and her soft cries as he raked her with his tongue. Again and again until she was squirming beneath him, begging for him to make her come.

He flicked his tongue against the hooded center of her, featherlight movements at first, then when her fingers curled in his hair and pulled, urging him on, he laved her in purposeful circles, applying a deliberate pressure to take her where he wanted her. *She was close, so close.* He plunged his fingers back inside of her and her scream rang out in the night.

"Oh, God." She pressed her hands to her face, her body supine beneath his, her chest rising and falling rapidly. He crawled his way up her body, stripped her hands from her face and kissed her until she tasted his dominance.

He lifted his mouth long moments later and surveyed her hazy gaze. "You still need to soothe the beast."

Her delicious mouth parted. "How might I do that?"

He ran a finger down her cheek. "I want you on top of me, riding me, until there's nothing left in me. And then," he added deliberately, "you can do it again."

Sofía had never been so turned on in her life. Nik was like a cat who'd escaped his pen tonight, desperate to possess her, single-minded in his intent. It made her feel delicate and feminine and oh, so hunted.

She ran her finger along his bottom lip. He closed his teeth around it and tugged, pulling a smile from her lips. "That would require great stamina. Is the king up to it?"

He took her hand and brought it to his groin, closing her fingers around his thick erection. "What do you think?"

Electricity rocketed through her. He was so big, so

rampantly male. The thought of having him inside her after all these weeks was unbearably exciting.

She pushed a hand against his chest. He moved obediently off her, his gaze tracking her as she slid off the bed and shrugged her shoulders to send her dress slithering to the floor. The expression on Nik's face made her tremble. He looked as if he wanted to devour her whole.

Nik joined her, stripping off his pants and boxers. He sprawled on the bed, spreading himself out like an olive-skinned feast for her personal consumption. His impressive erection was impossible to ignore, skimming the taut, defined wall of his abdomen. *He looked as if he might last forever...*

She climbed on the bed and straddled him, her hair sliding against his muscular chest as she brought her mouth down to his. She kissed him, feasted on him until he captured a chunk of her hair in his fingers and lifted her mouth from his.

His eyes were a hot, feverish blue, burning with intent. He fisted himself and brought the wide tip of his erection to her hot, damp flesh. Just the touch of him sent an excited shiver through her. She lifted her hips to take him inside her; gasped as he palmed her buttock and arched his hips, filling her with his thick, hard length in one savage thrust.

She rested her palms on his abdomen, eyes closed as she absorbed the sensation of being impaled on him. When the world righted itself, she opened her eyes.

"You are an animal tonight."

"Too long," he growled. "It's been too long."

His fingers gripped her hips. He lifted her off him, then back down, filling her with his hard, hot possession. Blinding her to anything but what it was to be taken by him, body and soul. Because that's what this was, no matter what either of them said, wanted to admit to each other, this was far beyond sex.

A moan escaped her. He gave her no reprieve, pulling her down on him again and again, his rough commands to take him deeper, harder, more animalistic than they'd ever been before.

Her body stirred back to life at the feel of him everywhere. He was that big, that powerful in this position. *Indescribable.*

He wrapped a hand around her jaw, his eyes blazing a path right through her as he brought her mouth down to his. There was a fierce need for possession in his eyes, but there was also a hunger. A hunger so deep she felt it down to her toes.

He wanted her. He needed her. But there was more. A depth of emotion he couldn't hide.

Witnessing it evoked dangerous thoughts. The thought that maybe, someday, he could get past his lack of trust. Be able to *love* her. Because she was afraid that's what she was beginning to want.

His tongue raked her bottom lip, demanding entry. She opened for him as he thrust it inside, mimicking the hard drives of his body. Her flesh softened, melted around him, giving him everything he asked for. He continued his merciless assault until his breath came in harsh pulls and his big body tensed, poised on release.

He slid his hand between them then, the rough pad of his thumb finding her core. He circled against her, his breath hot on her cheek as they came up for air. Sofía moaned, low and desperate.

"That's it, *agapimeni*," he urged, "come with me."

His expert touch, his hard driving body pushing her closer with every stroke tumbled her into a sweet, deep release that washed over her like a powerful tide, radiating outward from where his thumb played her. She uttered a strangled groan as it racked every nerve ending.

Nik growled, took her mouth and ground against her as he sought his release, the friction pulling her orgasm out in an extended, exquisite shudder.

The hot clench of her body pushed him over the edge. He drove harder, his essence spilling into her in a sweet, hot rush. She wrapped her legs tighter around him, savoring him.

When their breathing slowed, Nik pulled her down to nestle against his chest. She rested her head against the hard thud of his heart as he stroked her hair. It slowed gradually to an even, regular beat beneath her ear.

The connection they shared, the perfection of it, brought a question tumbling from her mouth.

"Who was she, Nikandros?"

CHAPTER TEN

NIK'S HAND STILLED on her hair. "Who are you talking about?"

She pushed herself up on her forearms to look at him. "The woman who's made you so gun-shy. So mistrustful. Stella told me about her, but she wouldn't give me details."

A flat, self-contained expression moved across his face. "She was nothing."

"If she was nothing, then you can tell me."

"Why?" Antagonism invaded that cool composure. "Why dredge up old history?"

"Because it goes to the heart of your mistrust of women. And I need to know."

He lifted her off him and set her on the bed. Sitting up, he raked a hand through his hair. "There isn't much to say. I dated a woman in my early twenties. I was less guarded back then. I shared things with her I shouldn't have. Near the end, when our relationship was coming to its natural conclusion, she could sense it and used some of the things I'd told her against me and my family."

She frowned. "What do you mean 'used them' against your family?"

"She sold a tell-all story to the press about our relationship. In it she revealed intimate details about my family."

"What details?"

"About my father's indiscretions."

Her heart sank. *Oh, Lord.* No wonder Nik held such a severe mistrust toward women. No wonder he'd accused her of doing anything she could to hang on to their relationship when a woman had done *that* to him.

She shook her head. "She is one woman, Nik. *One* woman out of the greater majority who would never be so vengeful, so spiteful as to do something like that to you. Surely you understand most people are more trustworthy than that?"

"Are they?" A dark brow winged its way upward. "I have never been with a woman who didn't want me for something, Sofía. Some are simply power hungry. To walk into a room on the arm of a prince holds great appeal. To enjoy my personal fortune in a city like New York does as well. Their intentions might not all have been as vengeful as Charlotte's, but they all wanted something from me. That's the way women work."

Her shoulders stiffened, her gaze raking over his face. "*I* didn't."

He said nothing.

Blood pounded her head. He was never going to believe her. He was always going to paint her with that brush.

She slid off the bed before her anger consumed her. "I'm going to shower."

"Sofía—"

She waved a hand at him, continuing her headlong flight toward the bathroom. She was almost there when he caught up with her, his fingers digging into her biceps to spin her around. "*Thee mou*, but you are a recalcitrant creature."

"*Recalcitrant?* Are all women children to you, too, Nik?"

He cupped the back of her head, his eyes blazing. "What do you want me to say?"

"I want you to say you know I am different. That you know I could not have planned that pregnancy. That that isn't me." She lifted her chin. "Did I *ever* at any point in our relationship lead you to believe I wanted to hang on to you past our *due date*? That I wasn't playing by the rules?"

"That last night," he said in a clipped tone. "You were different. I think you were getting emotionally attached. You were ending it because you were afraid you were going to get hurt."

She stared at him. Caught red-handed because it was true.

"You know what, Nik, you're right," she agreed, knowing one of them had to end this game of chicken they were playing. "I was ending it that night because I was falling for you. Even though I told myself it was unwise, that I knew the rules, I thought somewhere in us, in that *complexity* you threw around the other night, we had something special. That it was beyond sex. That we were *different*. There was no planning. No *scheming* to make a baby. And *that* is the truth."

He said nothing for a long moment, clearly caught off guard. She studied the emotion darkening his eyes. "What's the matter?" she taunted. "Does it unnerve you that I care? That I think we have the potential to be more?"

"No," he said, after a long moment. "I think we need *more* to have a good relationship."

"Then what?"

He rubbed his palms against his temples. "I think maybe I've been wrong."

"About what?"

"About you. About you engineering this pregnancy. I made that accusation based on experiences, situations I've faced which have taught me that people can't be trusted, Sofía. That I can't *afford* to trust people. When I found out you were pregnant, it was a natural assumption for me to think it had been planned, considering how careful we had been never to let that happen. Perhaps not a *right* one, but the *one* way I've become conditioned to think."

She crossed her arms over her chest and gave him a mutinous look. "Contraception is not foolproof, Nik. I had no idea the medication I was on would have interfered with it or I would certainly never have suggested what I did."

"It was my responsibility, too," he admitted. "I could have used a condom. I didn't."

She bit her lip. "Why this sudden change of face? Why now?"

He shook his head. "Because it isn't you, Sofía. My head's been a mess from my brother's death. From everything that's been thrown at me. I wasn't thinking straight. When I did start thinking clearly again, it just didn't seem like you. You are so fiercely independent and honest. It seemed like you were fighting it too hard to have wanted it. But I didn't have the head space to process those thoughts. I didn't want to be wrong again and trust someone when I shouldn't."

She pursed her lips. "And now you've had time to process it?"

"Yes."

Suspicion warred with a desperate need to know he

believed her. She shook her head. "You *have* to trust me, Nik. You have to let me in. You have to know that I *am* different."

His mouth thinned. "I just shared with you an incident that nearly broke my family apart. I told you about my father earlier. We are *talking*, Sofía. I can't promise it's always going to be easy for me or I'm always going to be perfect at it, but I am giving it my best shot."

Her heart softened. He *had* been trying. Had been opening up slowly, piece by piece. She knew in her heart they could make it together if he'd just continue to let her in. If *she* could continue to let him in. They had so much to build on.

She stepped closer to him. "You promise I'm not going to wake up tomorrow with you doubting me again?"

"I promise." He slid an arm around her waist and pulled her close. "*Lypamai.* I'm sorry. I'm sorry my suspicions have made this so difficult for us."

She held his gaze with hers. "*Everything* for me right now is based on me trusting you. On taking a leap of faith that petrifies me, Nik. I need to know I can rely on you. That you will be there for me."

He brought his mouth down on hers in a whisper-soft caress that drained any remaining anger from her. "You can jump," he murmured. "I will catch you. You are right, Sofía. We are *more*. We can be a good team. I promise you."

Team. It was a vivid reminder of who she was marrying. A man who might have just promised to build a relationship with her, who liked and desired her, but who would never love her. Nothing had changed there. He had married her to secure his heir.

She vowed to remember that as her lips clung to his and the kiss moved deeper. This time their coming together wasn't about urgency or release, it was about leisurely exploring each other, about sealing a promise they were making. To do this together.

She sighed and sank back into the wall, her palms coming up to cup his face. He inserted a knee between her thighs and moved in closer, deepening the kiss. He had never really lost his erection. It lengthened, thickened against her now. Pulsed with his desire for her.

He wrapped his fingers around her thigh and hooked it around his waist. She pulled in a breath as he nudged the tender flesh between her legs with his shaft. "Sore?" he asked.

"Yes."

He buried his mouth in the hollow of her throat. "I'll be gentle."

"Yes."

He eased himself inside of her. Her body drew him in. He rocked against her, his eyes holding hers as he fused them together. Slowly, with heart-stopping tenderness, he took her. Higher, deeper until her sensitized body stirred back to life.

The struggle she saw in his eyes gave her hope. He didn't want to want her this much. He was fighting the connection they had. Fighting what they had always had that had seemed to be bigger than both of them. Out of their control.

It scared her too, *terrified* her. But she needed him to be her anchor in this. Knew that he would be even if he never loved her. And that had to be enough.

He surged inside of her again and again with deliberate precision, the friction of his body against her flesh almost painfully good. She came apart on a long, delicious surge of pleasure, her fingernails digging into his biceps. Nik groaned, clasped her hips tighter and came inside of her, the skin of his beautiful face pulling taught as the pleasure consumed him.

Their breathing slowed. Her legs slipped to the floor. The haze of passion enveloping her lasted throughout the hot shower Nik set her under and until he tucked her into the big, luxurious bed. As she drifted off to sleep she curled against his chest.

She didn't want to think about the jump she'd just taken. The stakes that had been raised, just as she'd known they would be tonight. The fact that if she crashed this time, it would be a far bigger fall than the last.

Two sun-soaked days passed, and with it Sofía's hope for her and Nik grew. They ate delicious food, played in the sea and indulged in an endless amount of lovemaking that had her convinced her fiancé had the stamina of four men.

It was the time they'd needed to be able to focus on one another away from all the pressure. It had made all the difference in the world. Slowly, Nik was opening up to her. He was still guarded. He would likely always be guarded given his past, but less defensive when she probed, as if he was learning the rules of a game he'd never played. But then again, so was she. In that way, they were perfect for each other.

What worried her, she thought pensively as she watched Nik return from a sail on their final day in Evangelina, his lithe, beautiful body as he secured the boat a major distraction from the sketch pad in front of her, was when they returned to their stressful life tomorrow where Nik literally carried the weight of a nation on his shoulders. Where she was going to have to face the forces that awaited her and somehow not let them destroy her. She feared their progress would be sorely tested.

And that wasn't even counting the part of her that knew she was falling in love with Nik, something that made her feel like crawling out of her skin. So vulnerable she felt raw and exposed. But she'd promised herself she was going to see this journey through. She was stronger than this as Nik had reminded her the night of their engagement party. She could do this for the sake of her child. And maybe, just maybe, she would end up with far more than she'd bargained for with Nik.

She looked down at her sketch pad rather than let that thought fester. Examined her latest drawing. *Still not right.* Yet again. Grimacing, she tore the sheet off, crumpled it into a ball and added it to the growing pile beside her lounge chair.

Dammit. Why wasn't it coming? All those ideas she'd had in her head weren't translating to the page. She picked up her cool lime drink and attempted to channel some Zen.

Boat secured, Nik loped up the beach and dropped down on the chair beside her. Plucking the glass out of her hand, he drained its contents and set it on the concrete. Her mouth curved. "Is there anything you think is *not* yours?"

His eyes glittered in the sunshine. "No. Did I not prove that last night? Do you need a reminder?"

Her chin dipped, a wave of heat descending over her that had nothing to do with the sun. "What I *need* is for one of these designs to work."

He picked up one of the balls of paper. "May I?"

"Will you be honest?"

He lifted a brow as if to say when hadn't he been?

"Go ahead, then. I'm working on a maternity line."

He unballed one of the drawings, then another. Until he'd looked at them all. Twice. A frown of concentration creased his brow. "Well," she said, teeth buried in her lip. "What do you think?'

He looked up. "Qualifying this with the caveat I know nothing about fashion, I agree they're missing something."

"Inspiration," she murmured. "Nothing's hitting me."

He sat back in the chair, sprawling his long limbs out in front of him. "I think you're doing a typical Sofía. You're going for the safe choices—what you think people will like, *approve of*, instead of giving your imagination free rein. You're not fully committing."

"I am," she protested. "I've been killing myself over these."

He gave her a look as if to say that was exactly her problem. "Draw something for yourself. Draw something crazy, way over the top to get your creative juices flowing. You can always pull it back."

She eyed him. "Where do you get all this creativity expertise?"

"You'd be surprised at the amount of creativity it takes to put a ten-million-dollar deal together, *agapi mou*." He lifted himself off the chair. "Try it."

She chewed on her pencil as he went off to shower. Considered her surroundings and how the lush beauty of the island, the intensity of the colors, the smells inspired her. She started drawing and didn't stop until Nik came to get her for dinner.

"Any success?"

"Yes," she said, snapping the sketch pad closed.

"You going to share?"

"Not yet. They still need lots of work. But I'm happy with them. I think this is the direction I want to go."

"Good." He pointed her toward the villa. "Then I can have your undivided attention over dinner."

Nik's undivided attention proved as heady and fascinating a thing as always. But her head kept skipping forward to what lay ahead, distracting her.

Nik pointed his wineglass at her as their entrée plates were removed. "Where is your head?"

"I don't want to go back," she admitted. "I wish we could just stay here. Away from all the pressure."

"You aren't marrying a normal man, Sofía. You're marrying a king."

She sighed. "I know. Just wishful thinking."

"Come show me your drawings."

She gave him a pointed look. "I told you they aren't ready."

"I'll make it worth your while."

She pretended to think about it. But the temptation was too great. Pushing her chair back, she grabbed her sketch pad and walked around the table. Nik pulled her onto his lap, settling her against his chest.

"I want the truth," she reminded him, then flicked open the sketch pad and showed him the series of ten drawings she'd decided on, which still needed to be filled out and perfected, but they were a start. She talked him through each one, why she'd done what she'd done, what she liked about them. Nik studied them, then set the sketch pad down.

"I like them. They're elegant. Different."

She chewed on her lip. "You really like them? You're not just being nice?"

"You're a sure thing," he murmured. "Why would I be nice?"

Her mouth fell open. She was about to give him a knock across the head when she saw the sparkle in his eyes. "You are *terrible*."

"Sometimes you need to lighten up." He nuzzled her

cheek, the stubble on his jaw razing her skin. "I think they're great."

She rested her head against his chest, absorbing his warmth. He ran a hand over her hair. "Things are going to get crazy, Sofía. They always do. When it happens, when it feels as if we are surrounded by a force far greater than us, remember we can do this."

A sense of foreboding slid through her. "You make it sound so easy."

"It won't be. But you are up to the challenge, *agapimeni*. I have no doubt."

She hoped she was. Thought she might be. Guessed she was about to find out.

CHAPTER ELEVEN

NIK SLID INTO his car on a bright, sunny afternoon in Akathinia, a peace treaty with Carnelia in hand. A series of meetings between the two countries in the weeks following his return from Evangelina had finally borne fruit as he and Idas had signed the treaty and begun to map out plans for an economic alliance.

Because he didn't fully trust the Carnelian king, Nik had also pushed the development of an enhanced military force forward, but it would take months to see real progress on that initiative given the scale and coordination involved. Meanwhile, he would continue to push the alliance forward with his neighbor by putting a framework in place.

Bringing the Jaguar rumbling to life, his favorite toy to taunt his detail with on the windy, coastal roads, he took the scenic route home to the palace. The sense of well-being that settled over him was profound. His press conference to announce the peace treaty had inspired a feeling of relief and celebration among Akathinians. He could now get on with the business of running this country and looking toward the future rather than the perpetual crisis control mode he'd been in since he'd become king.

The sparkling Ionian Sea to his right, the spectacular

peaks of the Akathinian hills to his left, it was hard not to appreciate what destiny had handed him in that moment. He felt content. It felt *right*, as if what Sofía had said was true. That perhaps it was his destiny to lead Akathinia at this stage of its history.

Part of that had come with letting go of his life in New York. *Truly* letting go of it. He couldn't live with his head in both places. He'd had to choose. It didn't mean he would never grieve his former life. It wouldn't be human for him not to. But as he got more comfortable in his role as king, the affinity he'd always felt toward his homeland had taken over. He *knew* he could take this country where it needed to go. Knew he had the global perspective his father and Athamos had not.

If he was content, his fiancée was another reason for it. Having her back in his bed, having that intimate bond to look forward to every evening made the long, complex days bearable. They'd taken to having dinner together in their suite a couple of nights a week so they could spend quality time with each other. He'd found himself sharing more and more of his thoughts and plans with Sofía as the days went on. Her sharp, objective perspective on things always gave him excellent food for thought.

Thankfully, his soon-to-be wife also seemed to have found a peace of her own. When she wasn't doing a public appearance with his mother or sister, she was caught up in her designing with a ravenous enthusiasm that made him smile.

They'd given a joint interview to Akathinian TV last week, their first broadcast interview together. Sofía's inner happiness had shone through this time, her innate wit and charm capturing the host's heart and earning her good reviews. The image-conscious press had also picked up on her fashion sense, grudgingly conceding she was a bit of a shining star.

It was the boost of confidence Sofía had needed. She was acting more like her charismatic self, the woman he'd known in New York. And if that took him dangerously close to exploring uncharted feelings for his soon-to-be wife, he had deliberately held a part of himself back for just that reason. Now was not the time to be clouding his head with emotions he wasn't capable of fully expressing. Feeling.

He had promised Sofía a partnership. To protect her, to be by her side. For a man who didn't do commitment this was one promise he could keep.

They were done. Sofía stood back and surveyed the ten prototypes she'd created for the maternity line she would launch at the boutique, pride swelling her heart. It wasn't a whole line, but it was ten solid pieces to start the fall/ winter collection with next year. Ten pieces Katharine had raved about and couldn't wait to sell.

A rather ridiculous number of customers had come in to the boutique asking for the dresses Sofía had worn in her public appearances. The press coverage she had once considered a suffocating fishbowl was paying dividends. The sooner she got these prototypes off to the manufacturer so they could source material for them and produce samples for approval, the better to take advantage of the current buzz surrounding her and Nik's engagement.

Satisfaction at a job complete filling her, she leaned back against a table and drank in the late-afternoon sunshine pouring through the windows of the studio. She felt remarkably content. She'd given up her obsession with what the people thought of her because she really couldn't control that and focused instead on her design work and the creative outlet it provided.

The restlessness that had consumed her since coming to Akathinia had faded as she'd gained a sense of purpose. When she was using her role for good as she had when she'd visited Stella's youth group and shared her experiences in business, when she helped Queen Amara with one of her charitable endeavors, she could see a vision for her life here.

It helped that she and Stella had become fast friends. Although Queen Amara had taken Sofía under her wing and guided her in her role, she had the sense the queen would always have a certain distance about her, just as Nik had said. As if she held part of herself back. Perhaps it was her way of protecting herself against the storms and humiliations she had endured with her husband?

And then there was Nik. Her insides warmed as they always did when she thought about him. Her cynical, hard fiancé was evolving into a more knowable, approachable version of himself as they continued to deepen their bond. It made her decision to gamble on them, to gamble on the fact he might develop deeper feelings for her someday seem as if it hadn't quite been the foolish thought it had seemed at the time. That capturing his heart was within the realm of possibility.

Heavy footsteps sounded in the hallway. Her heartbeat picked up in anticipation. *Nik home already?*

Her suspicion was confirmed as her fiancé walked in, a dark suit complementing his swarthy good looks, a sexy aura of satisfaction surrounding him. She smiled a greeting. "I saw the announcement. Congratulations."

He crossed the room and gave her a kiss. "*Efharisto.* It feels good." He waved a hand at the prototypes as he released her. "What's this?"

"My first ten designs," she said proudly. "I'm about to ship them off to a manufacturer to get samples made."

"That's exciting."

"It is. I think we should celebrate."

He subjected her to a lazy inspection that bumped her pulse up a notch. "A personal celebration in our rooms later, to be sure, *agapimeni*, plus I thought I'd take you out to dinner. I have something I want to show you."

She *loved* that idea. "Give me a few minutes to change."

They dined at a tiny local seafood restaurant along the coast that was known to serve the best food on the island. Then they got back into Nik's car and drove another few miles to the rugged, most scenic east coast of the island, where the highest peaks of Akathinia dropped in a sheer cliff to the rocky shore below.

Sofía stepped from the car, her eyes widening as she took in the dramatic view and the remnants of the old fortress scattered along the edge of the cliff.

"What is this?"

Nik took her hand by way of answer and led her through the disintegrating ruins out to the edge of the cliff. "Carnelia," he said, pointing to a dark mass in the distance, lit by the dying rays of the sun. "This is where my great-grandfather King Damokles defeated the Catharian navy to secure Akathinia's independence. When they attacked us, the Catharians sent a smaller contingent to the harbor as a decoy knowing we would expect them to strike there, then massed most of their troops here. They bet on the fact my great-grandfather would mass his forces at the harbor to defend it, but Damokles was too smart to fall for that. He sent his best troops here, defeated the Catharians, and they retreated, never to come back."

Sofía stood there quietly, taking it in. The significance of where they were standing, what it meant to Nik slid over her, giving her goose bumps.

Nik pointed at the big cannons still guarding the cliff face. "Thousands of men lost their lives defending Akathinia that day. My great-grandfather said it was the bloodiest battle he'd ever been in."

She turned to him. "And you will never put your people through that again."

"If I can help it, no."

She studied the clear blue of his eyes. The strain seemed to have eased from his face with today's announcement. "I am so proud of you, Nik. You have been carrying the weight of a nation on your shoulders. Not an easy task in normal times. I hope you can relax a bit now. Give yourself some space to breathe."

He nodded. "It will be good to have that time. It's been difficult to process it all. To forge a plan for the future."

"And the responsibility that's been handed to you? Are you feeling more at peace with it?"

"Yes." He caught her hand in his and drew her close. "I need to thank you," he said quietly, "for being here for me. For telling me the things I needed to hear. For taking the risks you have. You inspire me, Sofía, your grit and determination to survive—to succeed."

A rush of warmth flowed through her. Her heart felt too big for her chest as she lifted a hand to his jaw. "You pushed *me* when I needed to be pushed. You made me realize I was living in fear. *I* should be thanking you for that, Nik. *I* of all people should know life is finite. I can't spend my days waiting for the penny to drop. For that bolt of lightning that might never come."

He inclined his head, his gaze softening. "We make a great team. I told you we would."

Team. She flinched at the word. They were more than a team, *dammit.* He *felt* things for her. Things he wouldn't address.

Nik's gaze sharpened on her face. "I care about you, Sofía. You know I do."

How much? The words vibrated from her across the crisp night air to him. They stayed there, hanging between them as both refused to break the standoff.

Was she completely deluding herself about how he felt? Would the wounds he carried only ever allow her so close?

She realized with a sickening feeling, in that moment, that she wasn't *falling* in love with him. She was *in love* with him. Had been ever since their weekend in Evangelina. Her heart lurching, she wondered how she had ever let that happen.

Sure she had to stop living in fear, but making herself that vulnerable to Nik of all people? A man who didn't even know what love was because he'd never been shown it? She had been bound and determined that night in New York to end it between them because she'd known this would happen. And now it had.

A grim look on his face, Nik snaked an arm around her waist and brought her to him. Her eyes fluttered closed as he kissed her. His usual tactic for fixing things between them. She remained unresponsive beneath the pressure of his mouth, too terrified to give him any more than she already had. When he finally let her go, she could feel the frustration emanating from him, an overwhelming force it would be all too easy to give in to. Instead she walked away, his muffled curse following her back to the car.

It had been bad enough when she hadn't loved him, these leaps he was asking her to make. This, *this* was just too much.

CHAPTER TWELVE

THE WHITE MALTESE stone Akathinian palace glittered in the sunlight as the helicopter dipped down over the sea and headed toward home. A strong headwind had been at their nose all the way back from Athens, increasing Nik's impatience, fueled by the news Sofía had given him on the phone last night.

She'd felt their baby kick for the first time. Hearing the wonder in her voice had turned his head into a hot mess.

Piero, his pilot, brought the helicopter in to land safely on the pad. Grabbing his briefcase, Nik stepped from beneath still-whirring blades and headed across the lawn toward the front steps to the palace he took two by two. Abram emerged as he reached the top step, his aide wearing that same frozen look he had the night he'd told him Athamos had died.

"What is it?"

"Idas has seized a ship in the Strait of Evandor."

His blood ran cold. "An Akathinian ship?"

"Yes. A warship doing exercises."

"It can't be Idas." His mind sped a mile a minute. "We have a peace treaty."

"The ship that took our vessel had Carnelian flags, Your Highness."

Thee mou. "Have there been any other reports of aggression?"

"Not that we've been able to ascertain."

It afforded him little comfort. His heart pounded as his brain funneled through procedure. "Call an emergency meeting of the Council, including the Joint Chiefs of Staff."

Abram nodded.

"I'll go by helicopter. Tell Piero to hold off."

He found his father and appraised him of the situation. Next he found Sofía in the salon with Stella, the two of them looking through magazines. She smiled when she saw him, but it faded when she saw the look on his face.

"Idas has taken an Akathinian ship in the Strait of Evandor," he said without preamble. "I'm on my way to meet with the Executive Council."

Sofía's eyes widened. "But you have a peace agreement in place."

Which meant nothing apparently. Idas had made a fool out of him.

Sofía got to her feet. "Maybe it's misinformation."

"The attacking ship bore a Carnelian flag." He pinned his gaze on his fiancée, a red mist descending over his vision. "Neither of you are to leave the palace until this situation is resolved."

"Have there been other attacks?" Stella asked.

"Not that we know of." Nik swung his gaze to his sister. "You still don't leave."

She nodded. He stalked to the door, so angry, *furious* with himself for being duped, he could barely see.

Sofía intercepted him at the door, her hand on his arm. "You don't have all the facts. It would be easy to jump to conclusions in this situation."

"Like Idas is a snake? That he broke his word?"

She blinked as he shouted the words at her. "Nik—"

He picked her up and moved her aside. She followed him into the hallway. "Do not let Idas drag you into a war you know is wrong. Listen to your instincts, now of all times."

He kept walking. *Listen to his instincts?* His instincts had been right all along.

The siege over the Akathinian warship taken in the Strait of Evandor lasted for forty-eight hours. Forty-eight nail-biting hours in which Sofía, Stella and Queen Amara paced the floors of the palace salon while Nik and a team of negotiators attended meetings in Geneva to free the ship and its crew, currently being forcibly held in Carnelian waters.

King Gregorios was ordered to bed when his blood pressure skyrocketed, something Sofía was inordinately grateful for. The elder king's vitriolic diatribe against Idas was only making a difficult scenario much, much worse.

Abram briefed them as he could. Nik was in the midst of a storm, with his Council divided on whether to provide a military response to retrieve the ship. Some felt enough was enough, Idas needed to be confronted. Nik was on the side of diplomacy, aware Akathinia's military was still heavily outmatched by its aggressors. He had refused to send negotiators to Geneva, insisting, instead, on being there himself and was doing his best to manage both sides of the equation.

The situation was not made easier by the reaction of the Akathinian people. Such an act of provocation on the heels of the crown prince's death could not be tolerated was the majority opinion. Get our men back.

Deep into the third day of the crisis, Abram appeared

in the salon to say it was done. Sofía's heart pounded as he announced the negotiations had been successful and the ship had been returned to Akathinian hands, but that five men had been killed in the taking of the ship.

When Nik walked into the palace hours later, dark circles ringing his eyes, Sofía, who had not slept for three days except for a couple of hours here and there, got to her feet, along with Stella and Queen Amara.

"Why did the Carnelians take the ship?" Queen Amara asked. "Why did Idas break his promise?"

Nik rubbed a hand across his brow. "They accused the ship of provocation toward one of its own. Clearly a fabrication, as our vessel was in neutral waters at the time, doing routine exercises."

His mother's gaze softened. "You must eat, Nikandros. Get some rest."

"I need to brief Father first." He flicked a glance at Sofía. "Go and eat. Don't wait for me."

She did, but the anxiety seizing her insides hardly inspired an appetite. Nik didn't join her in their rooms until well after eleven as she sat trying to read a book, but failing miserably.

"Did you eat?" she asked.

"I'm not hungry."

"Nik, you have to eat. Let me—"

"Don't." He held up a hand. "I'm fine."

He started undoing the buttons of his shirt, cursed as his fingers fumbled over them, then pulled the material apart with a hard yank, buttons scattering and rolling across the floor. Her stomach knotted. She put the book down, got to her feet and crossed to him. Ignoring her, he yanked his belt buckle open, freed the button on his trousers and shoved them down his hips.

"Nik." She moved closer as he stepped out of them. "Stop for a second. *Breathe.*"

He looked down at her, eyes blazing. "If I do, I will explode."

"It's not your fault. You can't blame yourself for this. You had every reason to believe Idas would keep his word."

"Did I?" He hurled the words at her. "Because in hindsight I feel like a fool. In hindsight he played me masterfully. He never intended on keeping that peace treaty."

She swallowed hard. "How did he think he would get away with that explanation? Surely it was clear the ship was in neutral waters."

"It's his claim a commander on the scene who considered the ship a threat made the call."

"Maybe that's the truth."

The curse he uttered snapped her head back. "We have a peace treaty, Sofía. He played me. Five men are dead because of my decisions. *My* naïveté."

Her insides twisted. "You were trying to avoid a war, Nik. You are doing everything you can to protect this country, but it can only happen so fast. No one can fault you for that."

"I could have been more *vigilant.* If I had listened to my instincts, I could have anticipated he'd do something like this. Instead I listened to everyone around me."

"You had to do that. You have a council and advisers for a reason."

He gave her a scathing look as if to say look where that'd gotten him. Then turned on his heel and headed for the bathroom.

She sat on a chair in the bedroom and waited for him. He was hurting. He felt he had to take responsibility for those men's deaths. He was the head of the armed forces.

The king of this country. It must be humiliating to be betrayed by Idas like that. But it didn't mean anything he'd done had been wrong. It had all been right.

Nik walked into the bedroom after his shower and pulled on a pair of boxers, barely sparing her a glance. "Go to bed, Sofía. You need sleep."

She stared at him, waiting, wondering what to do. He moved past her into the salon. The sound of the whiskey decanter being opened, the clink of ice hitting crystal and whiskey being poured filled the silence. The terrace doors clicked open, then shut. He needed time to process. To decompress. She should leave him alone. And for once she did. She was too exhausted not to.

She woke sometime later, something instinctively telling her Nik was not in bed. A look at the clock told her it was 2:00 a.m. Rubbing her eyes, she let them adjust to the darkness, then she slipped out of bed and went to find Nik. He was reclined in a chair on the terrace, the near-empty bottle of whiskey now sitting on the table beside him.

His eyes were glazed as she knelt down beside him.

"You need to sleep, Nik."

"I can't."

Her chest tightened at the haunted look on his face. She took his hands in hers. "I know you consider this your responsibility. I know you are angry at yourself for letting Idas make a fool of you. But you negotiated the release of those men. You sent them home to their families, Nik. Now you need to get some rest so you can deal with this tomorrow."

"Five men died today," he rasped. "More will follow if I don't handle this correctly."

"*Many more* will follow if you don't get some rest and get your head on straight." She shook her head. "I know it's painful to lose those men. But this is what you do. You make the tough decisions so the rest of us don't have to. But you can't do that if you're beating yourself up over a mistake, if you're too tired to think."

He turned his gaze back to the floodlit gardens. She knew what he wanted, but she wasn't leaving him alone.

She slid onto his lap. His face tightened. "Sofía—" She pressed her fingers to his mouth, took his hand and guided it to her stomach. To what had woken her. She thought maybe the baby had gone back to sleep when there was no movement beneath their fingers for a good five seconds. Then the kick came, fast and powerful.

Nik's eyes widened. The baby kicked again.

"This," she said to him, "is what you are doing this for. For your child. So that he or she will know the freedom your great-grandfather fought for. Stay the course, Nik."

His gaze lost its glassy look, dark emotion filtering through it as another kick came. "Sofía—"

She cupped his face in her hands and kissed him. Deep and slow and soulfully to banish the demons. He lifted a palm to cup the back of her head, returning the kiss with a hot fervor that told her she'd broken through.

She kissed him until they were all each other could see. Then he picked her up, wrapped her legs around him and carried her inside.

He laid her on their bed, stripped off his boxers and followed her down. Her heart pounded as he positioned himself between her legs, his heavy thighs parting hers. She closed her eyes, bracing herself for the explosive power of him because she was ready for him, always ready for him. Instead he worked his way down her body, lingering over the tiny swell of her stomach, waiting for another kick to come. Absorbing it with a reverent press of his lips, he moved farther down, between the heat of her thighs. His mouth found her most sensitive skin, laved her, licked her until she was crying out his name, begging for him.

Covering her with his heavy body, he sheathed himself inside of her in one powerful movement that stole her breath. The need to forget, the need to cleanse himself of what had happened chased their coupling. She wrapped her thighs around him and brought his mouth down to hers with fingers that cupped his head. He murmured her name hoarsely into her mouth as he plunged inside her again and again until there was only them, as deeply connected as two human beings could be.

Nik clasped her hips in his hands, angled himself deeper and took her hard and fast until his big body tensed and he came in a violent explosion of pleasure that rocked them both, Sofía's release coming quick on its heels.

Cradling her to his chest, Nik rolled onto his side, his palm on her belly. She curled into the heat of his body. Then there was only the sound of his deep, even breathing.

I need you to remember that when things get crazy. When it feels like we are surrounded by a force far greater than us. We can do this.

The promise Nik had made to her in Evangelina filled her head. They were in the center of the storm now, just as he'd predicted. Now they had to find their way out.

CHAPTER THIRTEEN

NIK ROSE EARLY the next morning, his meetings with the Executive Council on the Carnelian situation slated to start at eight and go late into the day. In the dim light slanting its way through the windows, he pulled on a pair of trousers and a shirt.

His head throbbed from the whiskey he'd consumed; his body ached from far too little sleep. He'd hoped by shutting his eyes for a few hours, the images of the five dead crewmen being carried off the rescued ship would stop torturing him, but they had been burned into his brain. He might be only the figurehead leader of the military, but he had done the training, knew the classic tenet that had been drilled into their heads as soldiers: sacrifice for the greater good. But the thought of returning those men home to their families in a box wasn't an emotion he'd been trained to process.

A fist formed in his chest. He buttoned his shirt up over it and swung a tie around his neck. His gaze drifted to Sofía asleep in their bed as his fingers fumbled over the knot. To feel their baby kicking last night had knocked some sense into him. Sofía had knocked some sense into him.

He needed to protect her and his child. He needed to protect Akathinia. Everything hinged on what he did next.

While he had been playing in the sun with Sofía, convincing himself he was smarter than Idas, convincing himself he could have it all, his enemy had been plotting his next move. Outsmarting him. Five men were dead because of it.

Perhaps his father had been right. Maybe there was no middle ground for a leader. Either you had complete focus on the job as his father had, to hell with the people in your life, or your distractions ruined you.

He yanked a jacket from the closet and slid it on. His emotions were too close to the surface right now. Too all over the place. He needed some distance between him and Sofía while he navigated this crisis. From emotions that were too strong to process.

It wasn't difficult. His meeting went late into the night as expected. When he returned home Sofía was asleep. The pattern went on for two weeks as he debated the question of Carnelia at Council. Those who wanted to deal Carnelia a warning blow to show Idas Akathinia wasn't available to take were numerous. Those who, like him, knew diplomacy was the only answer, a minority. There was no middle ground, he argued to the proponents of a warning blow. It would drag Akathinia into a war it didn't want and they would lose without its enhanced military force in place.

On the fifteenth morning of bitterly fought debate, he used his veto power at Council to dismiss military action and announced an international peace summit would be held in Akathinia in two weeks' time to discuss the Carnelian situation. Idas would be invited, but it would proceed regardless of whether he attended. Nik was banking on the fact the international community would have his back, particularly those powerful nations with whom Akathinia had colonial ties.

His veto in place, he dissolved the council and went home. Enough talk had happened. It was time to end this.

Dinner with Nik's family was a painful affair. Another day of negotiations about the Carnelian situation had meant another day without Nik, and with Stella out on a date, it had been just her and the king and queen at the table. As soon as dessert was served, she excused herself and climbed the stairs to bed, exhausted and miserable.

She knew she should try to sleep. She needed the rest. But she knew she wouldn't, so she headed instead to her studio to work.

The dress she'd been working on, a chic blue silk knee-length design, cut on the bias and forgiving for her thickening middle, beckoned from the table, pieces cut out and ready to be assembled. But the excitement she'd felt earlier for the dress didn't spark her usual creative urge.

How could she feel inspired when her relationship with Nik was falling apart? When he had spent the past two weeks avoiding her, saying no more than a handful of words to her before he resumed working or passed out, exhausted. Only one night had he woken her to make love to her. Once he had assuaged his frustration, he had slept again, leaving her emotionally and physically distanced.

Which was what he was doing. Distancing himself from her, shutting her out. She understood he was stressed, under immense pressure, but the unraveling of all the work they'd done broke her heart. What kind of a *partnership*, as he liked to call it, did they have when he wouldn't turn to her when he needed her the most? When he wasn't there for *her*?

Her vision clouded over. She blinked as hot liquid stung the backs of her eyes. Outside in the glittering harbor, lit up at night, the expensive yachts hosted million-dollar parties even as Nik struggled to prevent a conflict with Carnelia. She could tell herself he was leading Akathinia through its toughest times. That she couldn't expect them to be perfect right now. But she knew even when he figured this out, which he would, there would be another issue to take its place. And another. And he would continue to shut her out every time. Compartmentalize her.

It wasn't enough anymore, she realized. She couldn't settle for a partnership. She wanted more. She wanted all of him. She couldn't spend her days waiting for him to decide he cared. She'd done that her whole life with her mother. She wouldn't do it with him.

Desperate for a familiar voice, she picked up her cell phone and called Katharine. The call went to voice mail. She tossed the phone on the table and looked back out at the night.

"You should be in bed."

She spun around at Nik's deep baritone. He stood just inside the door, his jacket draped over his shoulder, leaning against the frame.

"It's not midnight," she noted, hating the bitter tone in her voice. "Was everyone passing out at the table?"

He eased away from the wall, tossed his jacket on a table and walked toward her. "I've called a summit of international leaders for two weeks' time in Akathinia. There will be no military action."

"You used your veto power?"

"Yes."

"Good." She twisted a chunk of her hair around her finger as he stopped in front of her. "I am sure the international community will band behind you."

"That is the hope."

Silence fell. He reached out and ran his thumb across

her cheek. She flinched away from his touch, her chin coming up.

A blaze of fire sparked in his eyes, but he banked it down. "You look exhausted, *agapi mou*. Is it the baby?"

A surge of fury bubbled up inside of her. She shook her head, attempting to contain it. Nik narrowed his gaze on her. "What?"

She yanked in a breath in an attempt to find calm, but it all came tumbling out. "You shut me out as if I don't exist for two weeks, while I *worry* about you, while I worry about what's going to happen, then you waltz in here and ask me why I look tired? Why I'm not myself? Did you ever stop to think at any point in this crusade of yours what this is doing to me, Nik? Did you even *care*?"

His jaw hardened. "I told you this was going to be all consuming. That I wouldn't be home much."

"*All consuming?* You haven't said ten sentences to me. You've tuned me out like the unnecessary complication you like to view me as instead of that *partnership* you offered."

"Would you prefer I woke you at midnight to give you an update?"

"*Yes.* At least I'd know you were okay. Instead I've relied on Abram to tell me how my fiancé is holding up."

Something she couldn't read flickered in his eyes.

"Unless," she amended, "it had been the two or three nuggets you chose to enlighten me with before you used me to assuage your frustration."

The glitter in his eyes sparked into a dangerous blue flame. "You were wholly into that, Sofía."

"*Yes, I was.* I wanted to comfort you, to connect with you so desperately, Nik, I would have done anything to make you feel better. Including letting you use me for sex."

He stepped closer, clenching his hands by his sides. "I did not *use* you for sex."

"Then what was it? Me comforting you the way I *do it best*?"

His lashes lowered. "I told you there would be difficult times. Times we had to get through together."

"*Together* being the operative word. Since then, you have demonstrated how that will work for us. How you will let me in when it pleases you to, then shut me out when you decide I'm getting too close." She lifted her chin. "It was never a real offer of intimacy, was it? I was just too stupid to figure it out."

"I *have* let you in."

"You *think* you've let me in. I'm sure you'd call it a superstar effort. But your fixation on proving yourself, on demonstrating to your father how wrong he is about you, how you have this all *under control*, leaves you with nothing left over for me or anything else."

His face tightened. "I am *focused* on preserving this country's freedom. My father has nothing to do with it."

"Really?" She shook her head. "I suggest you think long and hard on that. Because to me you're becoming more like him every day. You're becoming just as dictatorial, just as obsessed about the end goal. And to hell with everyone and everything in between."

His face tightened. "I could question your own selfishness, Sofía. Now is the time for you to be supporting me, when this country is in the biggest crisis of its history. And what are you doing? Giving me grief about *paying attention to you*."

A strangled sound left her throat. She threw her hands up in the air. "And what happens when the next crisis comes? And the next? Life is never going to be simple for us. You said that yourself. You asked me to stand beside you, to do this together. I have done that, Nik. I am playing queen-to-be to the very limits of my ability. But if you can't let me in, if I'm doing this by myself, it isn't going to work. I will not commit myself to a marriage, to a *life* with a man who isn't willing to share himself."

"You cannot *claim* these are ordinary circumstances, Sofía. The other things will be manageable."

"Not with you. You will compartmentalize me every time you need to. Bring me out to play when you so desire."

He blew out a breath. Turned to look out the window. When he looked back at her, his eyes were glazed with exhaustion. "You're being unreasonable. Get some sleep and we'll talk in the morning."

She bit her lip, desperately resisting the hot tears that blanketed her eyes. "I've spent enough of my life alone, Nik. Craving the love I never got. I won't do it with you. I won't put our child through a marriage, a life where I am miserable. You can't even manage a relationship with me, let alone a child."

His mouth flattened. A tear rolled down her cheek. He cursed and reached up to brush it away, confusion, wariness, darkening his eyes. "Sofía—"

"Yes, that's right," she interrupted. "I'm in love with you, Nik. I realized I was in love with you in Evangelina. And you knew it. You have cleverly leveraged it to get what you want and I have played right into your hands."

His gaze dropped away from hers. Her heart broke apart at the unspoken admission. He *had* known. And somehow that made it so much worse.

"Make up your mind," she said quietly. "Figure out whether you actually have a heart, Nik, and you can share it with me. Or let me go. It's your choice."

The damaged look in his eyes as he raised his gaze to hers tested her resolve. "I know you're damaged, Nik.

So am I. But I've stopped using that as an excuse to run away from how I feel."

She left him there and went to bed. It felt good to put an end to the misery. To know it wouldn't continue. If he rejected her now, at least she'd know. At least she'd save herself a lifetime of pain. And really, how much more could it hurt?

A whole hell of a lot more, her bruised insides told her. It was just beginning.

His confrontation with Sofía raging in his head, Nik avoided the whiskey bottle that had been calling to him a little too much lately and sought out fresh air instead. The palace gardens were quiet and peaceful, the night air crisp and clean. Unlike the frantic activity of the day with gardeners and machines buzzing relentlessly to keep the showpiece intact, the carefully manicured slice of heaven that covered ten acres was silent now, except for the breeze that came off the sea and rustled the leaves on the trees.

There was a place on the outskirts of the gardens, a lone bench that faced the sea, where he and Stella used to come when they were kids to escape their father's wrath. He headed toward it, found it unoccupied as it always was and lowered himself onto the worn wood, splaying his long legs out in front of him.

He rested his head against the back of the bench and closed his eyes. But the usual peace did not come. He couldn't deny every word Sofía had said was true. That he had known she was in love with him; that he had leveraged it for his own purposes. He had compartmentalized her to fit into his life because that was the only way he could operate. It wasn't something he was proud of, but he had accepted that particular transgression weeks ago. Forgiven himself for it.

But tonight, watching how miserable she was, when for a few weeks in time she had been so happy, tore him apart inside. He wanted her to be happy. *Needed* her to be happy after everything she'd gone through. He had promised he would be here for her, promised he would ensure that happiness, and then the Carnelian crisis had blown everything apart.

And that was a lie. He knew it as soon as the thought entered his head. Idas taking that ship, going back on their agreement, had made him question everything. Himself, the leader he'd become, whether he'd made the right choices, *whether he was cut out to be king*. But he'd made the decision to distance Sofía before that. When she'd gotten too close. When his feelings for her had become too strong.

Because making himself vulnerable, opening himself up fully to her, had meant abandoning his defenses, something he couldn't do because he wasn't actually sure he could function without them. Wasn't sure Sofía would even want what he had left inside. Wasn't even sure what was there anymore, he'd been closed off for so long.

He stared sightlessly out at the dark shadow of the water, the ironic truth of it all settling over him. *He* had been afraid. He had allowed fear to rule him while defiantly brave Sofía had taken every jump he'd asked her to. A woman he was afraid he'd been in love with for a long time.

He craved the peace she gave him. Knew she had the potential to heal the wounds inside of him. As she had done so again and again over the past few weeks, pulling him out of the darkness, steadying his path, convincing him to follow his heart. But he needed to pull his country back from the brink first. Solve this thing with Idas. Then he would address his relationship with Sofía.

The question was, did he have the capacity to offer her all of him? Or would he destroy her by making her stay?

CHAPTER FOURTEEN

"THE FIRST CAR will be here in thirty minutes, sir."

Nik turned to nod at Abram, who had appeared on the palace steps behind him. "Keep me posted."

With a dip of his head, his aide disappeared inside. Nik turned back to the sun-soaked harbor, bounded by the two Venetian fortifications that had once protected Akathinia from seagoing marauders. He was hoping today the international community would join forces to repel a very real and current threat to Akathinia's freedom in Carnelia.

Idas had, as expected, elected not to attend the peace talks, so the world would judge him in absentia.

He rubbed a hand to his pounding temple, operating on just about zero sleep after spending the past two weeks personally calling each and every one of the twenty-five world leaders in attendance today to persuade them to take the time out of their busy schedules to attend.

His gamble had paid off. A playground for the world's rich and famous, Akathinia was too bright a jewel of the Mediterranean, with too many colonial ties for its instability to be disregarded. All he had to do now was convince these powerful men to put their support on the table.

"They will be here soon?"

He turned to find his father making his way through the open front doors, moving slowly with his walking stick.

He nodded. "The first in thirty minutes."

His father stopped beside him, leaning heavily on the stick. "It is remarkable what you have done, Nikandros. I did not think this would happen."

What usually would have evoked bitterness, this inability of his father to believe in him, bounced off Nik without hitting its mark. He had been through too much these past few months, had endured too many highs and lows to continue to let it hurt. He knew what he was doing today was right. He was secure in his mind as the leader of this country. He only hoped it would wipe away the mistake he had made with Idas.

His father rested his gaze on him. "You have always been able to see the bigger picture. It is why you were successful in New York. In attracting the world to Akathinia. It's what you are building on today. Your connections, the relationships you have forged with these countries. It isn't something I nor Athamos could have done nearly as well."

"The world would not have abandoned Akathinia in its time of need."

"Perhaps not."

"It's not done yet. We could walk away from this with nothing."

"But you won't. The most powerful men in the world have not traveled here today to say they will not support you."

He surely hoped not.

His father fixed him with his steely blue gaze. "My grief has ruled me these past weeks. My anger. It is very easy to feel nothing but rage when your flesh and blood is taken from you. But I apologize if I have failed you, Nikandros. Not just now but in the past. You will learn, are *already* learning, that being a king is not easy. It will ask things of you you aren't prepared to give. Demand you make choices. Sometimes you will not always make the right ones."

How those words resonated in this moment. He fought the tightness in his chest at an apology issued decades far too late, resting his gaze on his father's. "I think I will make different choices. But I understand the complexity now perhaps much better than I did."

His father inclined his head. "I have always had equal respect for both my sons, but I fear I have not always shown it in the right way. Perhaps not much at all."

The fist in his chest grew. "That is in the past."

"Yes. Good luck today. I have every confidence you will be coming to me with good news."

Nik blew out a breath as his father leaned heavily on his stick and shuffled inside. Even when he'd told himself his father's opinion hadn't mattered, it had. It always had.

Sofía smoothed her hands over her hips as she surveyed her appearance in the mirror, a month's work staring her in the face.

Her dress. Her design. It was like exposing her insides to the world and hoping they loved her.

She turned to Stella. "What do you think?"

"Wow." The princess's gaze widened. "You look hot. Perfect, sophisticated, pregnant, queen-to-be hot."

Her stomach tightened. *If* she was to be queen. It had been two weeks since her and Nik's blowout. Two weeks since she had tossed her ultimatum in his face and her heart along with it. Two weeks in which he hadn't touched her, had spent all his time working on this summit while she worried they were done.

She bit her lip. "You're sure about the dress? If there's any doubt in your mind, I'll wear Francesco's."

Stella poked her in the shoulder. "There is no doubt in my mind. You are amazingly talented. Now grab your bag. We're late."

They were indeed late as they met the event liaison in the lobby of the palace for the photo op, to be followed by lunch with the wives of the foreign leaders. The buttoned-up, stern-looking woman frowned at them. "Everyone is gathered outside already."

"So we make a grand entrance," Stella came back mischievously, hooking her arm through Sofía's.

Sofía smiled through her misery as she and Stella stepped out into the bright Akathinian sunlight, the gods electing to greet their international guests with the country's usual golden splendor instead of the bizarre rain they'd had for the past week. Stella tugged her to a halt halfway down the steps. "Show off your dress."

The princess had a reputation for being a fashionista, too. The photographers swarmed to get a shot of her and Sofía, their flashes going off like mad.

"Stella. Is it true you are dating Aristos Nicolades?" a photographer yelled.

What? Sofía angled a look at Stella. "Tell me you're not."

The princess lifted a brow at the reporter. "Where do you *get* these ideas?"

Sofía's gaze flew to Nik, who stood at the bottom of the steps with the gathered contingent, his eyes fixed on his sister. His *furious* eyes. They glittered an electric blue in the sun, set off by his dark suit, crisp white shirt and ice-blue tie. When he turned them on her she went a bit weak at the knees at the banked intensity in them.

It took her right back to the night in New York at the Met when he had looked at her like that, the night that had set in motion a chain of events that had landed them here. And still she didn't know how it was going to end.

"Fabulous dress, Sofía," a photographer called out. "Who's it by?"

She lifted her chin, her heart swelling. "It's mine. I plan to launch a new line in my New York boutique next year."

"Would that be for a *maternity* line?"

She opened her mouth to fluff it off per usual, with the official announcement to come next week and who knew where she and Nik would be by then? Nik broke away from the crowd and climbed the steps to her side before she could find an appropriately evasive response.

"Yes," he said, slipping an arm around her waist. "Sofía and I are thrilled to say we are expecting our first child."

Stella choked out a sound beside her at the breach in protocol. The paparazzi went crazy with their cameras.

"What did you do that for?" Sofía demanded beneath her breath. "Now they're going to be a pack of wild animals."

"Because we *are* having a baby, *agapi mou*. It was getting painful watching you try to skirt the question."

She forced a smile to her lips as the flashes continued to go off. "Don't you think a press release is a better idea if we're not going to be together?"

He turned that ice-blue gaze on her. "I'm never letting you go, Sofía. *Ever*."

"You don't have a choice," she pointed out, maintaining her smile. "I told you I'm leaving after this if you don't let me in."

"That gives me twenty-four hours to change your mind."

She forgot about the cameras entirely, her heart tumbling to the concrete. "Nik—"

"Later," he growled, releasing her. "Unless you would like an audience for this."

No. No, she wouldn't.

They moved on to lunch. In the afternoon the leaders sat down once again to hash out a solution to the issue at hand. The palace PR person was called in to handle the communications crisis that erupted around the coming royal baby. By the evening news, the story was splashed across every news outlet on the planet with all kinds of sensational taglines attached to it. Jumping the Gun seemed to be a favorite, followed closely by Out of Wedlock Shock.

But the coming baby wasn't the only headline news. The fashion press went mad about Sofía's dress, calling it "ultrachic maternity wear" every design house would be duplicating by week's end.

After pouring through the masses of coverage the PR person gave her on her tablet, Sofía lifted her head, dazed. Finally she was a hit. Just in time for her and Nik's relationship to implode.

Nik walked out of the National Assembly as early evening fell, the political and military support of the international community behind him. If Carnelia acted against Akathinia, the world would respond. But Nik knew it wouldn't come to that. Not after the consensus of today made the news. Not after Idas realized his games were over.

He stopped to speak to the scrum of media waiting outside the Assembly. His PR person intercepted him on his way to the podium. "The news of the royal baby has gone viral. It's everywhere."

Tell him something he couldn't have predicted. He wasn't thrilled with himself for his impulsive move, aware his need to lay claim to Sofía could backfire badly on him if the media chose to focus on a royal baby rather than his country's political issues. But it was done now.

"Tell me some of the coverage has included the summit."

His PR person nodded, a smile curving her lips. "One of the big news channels was interviewing a pundit on the announcement. He joked Carnelia could hardly touch Akathinia now with a royal baby on the way. *Sacrilegious*, he called it. The clip was picked up everywhere."

His mouth slackened. "You're joking."

"I would not joke about something like that, Your Highness. Your fiancée is also being hailed as the next savior of fashion. They loved her dress."

That pulled a smile from him. Sofía had such high hopes for her maternity line but she wouldn't admit one of them.

He did the scrum alongside the superpower leaders, then headed back to the palace to change before the dinner and dance scheduled for that evening. The meeting had run long, which meant he had just enough time to change into formal wear before he and Sofía left for predinner cocktails in the palace ballroom.

His fiancée was standing in their dressing room putting a necklace on when he walked in. Her back was to him, her voluptuous body covered by a black, ankle-length gown that hugged every delectable curve. It left her entire back bare, the drape of the dress swooping to almost her waist.

It was one of the dresses from her sketches. She looked devastating.

Sofía glanced over her shoulder, necklace in hand, a frustrated look on her face. "I can't get this. Can you?"

He walked toward her and took the necklace, draping it around her slim neck and fastening it easily. When he was done, she went to move away. He closed his fingers around her upper arms, holding her there. "The dress looks amazing."

She kept her gaze focused straight ahead. "Nik—"

He dropped his mouth to her smooth, bare shoulder, inhaling the heady scent of her spicy perfume. "I told you I wouldn't let you go today because I *can't* let you go, Sofía. I need you here by my side, helping me navigate my way through this. Only with you do I feel at peace."

She froze, so motionless, so still, he tightened his hands around her shoulders and turned her around. Her big, dark eyes were full of apprehension and a misery that kicked him in the chest.

She pressed her hands to her cheeks. "I can't—I need more, Nik. It's not enough for you to need me, to *want* me, because you can turn it off and on like a switch and it breaks my heart every time you retreat."

"I know. *Lypamai. I'm sorry.*" He shook his head. "You make me feel things that terrify me. That challenge everything I thought I knew about myself. About what I am capable of. And still I want you, because what I once was, I'm not anymore. I don't want that solitary existence. I want you."

Her eyes were glued to his. "What feelings are you referring to?"

He reached for her hand and curled his fingers around hers. "You were right when you said I knew you were in love with me and that I used it against you. I was scared of the emotion I had for you, afraid of what giving in to my feelings would do to my ability to make critical decisions.

So I told myself a partnership was better for us. So I could deliver on my promise to protect you, to take care of you. But then my feelings got involved and I hurt you. I didn't think I could offer you what you needed, so I backed off."

He shook his head. "I should have known it was never going to work. My feelings for you were too strong. It's why I hadn't broken things off with you in New York. Because I was beginning to care."

She frowned. "You told me you were going to cut it off."

"I hadn't given myself an end date, Sofía. That says something."

"Oh, it certainly does," she growled. "I was a possession you wanted to hang on to a bit longer. My expiration date hadn't come up. And now you want to do the same but this time because I'm carrying your child."

"No. Because I *love* you." He tightened his fingers around hers. "You asked me that night to figure out whether I have a heart, whether I could share it with you. I honestly didn't know. I've kept myself closed off for so long I didn't know what I had left in me. And then you threatened to walk away and I knew. I knew I didn't want to do this without you. That I loved you. *Yes*, I want our baby, but it's *you* I need, Sofía."

Her eyes darkened to almost black, a suspicious brightness forming in them. "What about the next crisis? And the next? I can't keep going through this vicious cycle with you."

"You won't have to. I exorcised some demons today. That need to prove myself to my father you pointed out? My need to live up to my brother's memory? Everything led to that, you were right." He shook his head. "I'm never going to be perfect, but I know now I can move on. I can focus on the present. *You*," he said huskily. "Our baby. A future I never thought I'd have."

A tear slid down her cheek. "I have been so miserable the past couple of weeks. I thought you were done with us. I thought we were over."

"We are never over," he growled. "I had to make sure my head was on straight before we had this conversation. I didn't want to make promises I couldn't keep."

"And you're sure now?"

He pulled her closer, his hands settling against her silky, bare back. "Sure. Take one more jump with me, Sofía. I promise you won't regret it."

She drifted closer to him, her dark eyes softening into that molten brown fire he loved to watch. "Is that an order, Your Highness?"

He shook his head. "No more orders. I just need you to love me."

She stood on tiptoe and brought her mouth to his. "I do, Nikandros Constantinides. More than I should."

He took her lips in a soft, seductive caress that promised her everything he had. When he lifted his mouth, she was breathless. "You still, however, need to be punished."

She frowned. "For?"

"Your Highness…"

She started to laugh, a sound he'd never been so happy to hear. "Later. We're late."

He picked her up by way of response and deposited her on the dresser. Kissed her again. This time their kiss was needy and hot, their mouths and fingers rediscovering sacred territory. He cupped her backside and pulled her to the edge of the dresser, needing to seal their pledge with the shattering intimacy only they could produce.

"Nik," she breathed, "we *can't*."

"*Can't*," he said, "is not a word in my vocabulary."

Her fingers found his belt buckle. Pulling it open, the button and zipper on his pants followed.

"I love you," she whispered as she arched her hips and took him deep.

He rested his forehead against hers and said those three words to her again and again until her body contracted around his and she took him to heaven.

He'd been given a second chance. He didn't intend to waste it.

Nik and his queen-to-be slipped into the cocktail hour with the other international leaders fifteen minutes late. Their absence and the blush on Sofía's cheeks were duly noted, as was her gown, which was another smash hit.

Nik stood back and watched his fiancée shine as the paparazzi flashes went mad. Her dazzling smile made his chest tighten. The king had found his heart and it was standing right in front of him.

EPILOGUE

Sofía Ramirez married Nikandros Alphaios Constantinides on a bright, sunny, perfect Akathinian day in October in the breathtakingly beautiful royal chapel that had blessed every set of royal nuptials since the monarchy's inception over two centuries ago.

Five months pregnant in her Francesco Villa strapless white satin wedding gown, featuring a three-tiered, hand-appliquéd lace overlay of different shades of ivory, HRH Queen Sofía, Duchess of Armendine, made her way down the chandelier-lit marble aisle to join her intensely handsome groom, dressed in full military regalia.

She walked down the aisle by herself behind Katharine and Stella, her two bridesmaids, dressed in elegant ice-blue gowns. It only seemed right to leave her father's place empty, because nothing could ever replace him. Her blossoming relationship with her mother, however, was something she had come to treasure as it grew with every day that passed. Sometimes things *did* change.

The Akathinian television commentators covering the royal nuptials continued to warm to their new queen as she exchanged vows with her king.

"Regal and stunningly beautiful, Sofía has blossomed in her role," they said. "Clearly she has captured the heart of our king and is well on her way to capturing the heart of the people. Although I think the real show today," the reporter added with a smile, "was watching Nikandros's face as his bride walked down the aisle."

The couple left the chapel hand in hand to the uplifting strains of Beethoven's *Ode to Joy*, retiring to the balcony of the palace to address the massive crowds. After providing a particularly passionate kiss for the photographers, something that was becoming their trademark, they were recognized with a twenty-one-gun salute.

It wasn't until they were seated at the head table in the palace ballroom, surrounded by every manner of global royalty and celebrity, that Sofía took her first real breath of the day. It had been a wonderful one, her happiness with Nik a living, breathing entity that seemed to grow stronger with every day. But she would be happy when it was just the two of them back in Evangelina on the weeklong honeymoon they had planned.

As the guests settled in, their champagne glasses full in the sparkling candlelight, Nik rose to give a toast. After thanking everyone for coming in both English and his native language, he expressed his gratitude to the Akathinian people for working through the past few trying months with him.

Following the peace summit, the international community had thrown its full support behind Akathinia and Idas had backed off his inflammatory rhetoric in the press. Should Carnelia elect to resume its opportunistic hostilities toward its smaller neighbor, Akathinia would not be alone. Nik worried the threat from the aggressive Carnelian king was not over, but a sense of calm and ordinary life had settled over the island. And for now, it was enough.

"To peace," Nik said, lifting his glass.

The guests raised their flutes and drank, a quiet gratefulness filling the air at the preservation of the independent, tranquil life they valued so deeply. Then Nik turned to his bride.

He was eloquent in his toast to her, as a man who had addressed the United Nations was wont to be, but it was his final words that drew Sofía's first tears of the day.

"I did not know how love could change a man," he said, his gaze on hers. "How much better it could make me be, until I met you, Sofía. You are my heart. *Always*."

They left the reception by helicopter in the wee hours while the guests still celebrated, the lights of Akathinia glowing beneath them as they rose high in the air. When they were close to landing on Evangelina, Nik held out his hand. "Ready?"

Nodding, she joined him at the open doorway, a bouquet of lilies in her hand that matched the bouquet Nik carried. One for her father, one for Athamos. They had not been here, but they had not been forgotten. Timing their throw, they sent the flowers scattering across the sea.

The tears came again for Sofía, silent and bittersweet. "Thank you," she murmured, wrapping her arms around Nik's neck. "That was perfect."

His eyes were as full of emotion as she'd seen them. "He knows," she whispered. "He knows."

He kissed her then as the helicopter swooped toward their hideaway. Clutching the lapel of his sexy military uniform, she held on to the moment as long as she could. These days she was living for the present, knowing with Nik by her side, no matter what arrived to test them, it would never fall apart.

Their time together in Evangelina was always perfect. She intended to make the most of every last magical second of it.

* * * * *

The drama and passion of
KINGDOMS & CROWNS *continues in*
CLAIMING THE ROYAL INNOCENT
Available in May 2016
And look out for the final installment of
the trilogy coming soon!

MILLS & BOON®

MODERN™

POWER, PASSION AND IRRESISTIBLE TEMPTATION

0316/01

MILLS & BOON®

Helen Bianchin v Regency Collection!